A MAN OF HONOR

Theodor Fontane

A MAN OF HONOR

(Schach von Wuthenow)

TRANSLATED,
WITH INTRODUCTION
AND NOTES, BY

E. M. Valk

Frederick Ungar Publishing Co. : New York

Translated from the original German

Schach von Wuthenow

Copyright © 1975 by E.M. Valk
Printed in the United States of America
Designed by Irving Perkins

Library of Congress Cataloging in Publication Data
Fontane, Theodor, 1819–1898.
    A man of honor (Schach von Wuthenow).

    Translation of Schach von Wuthenow.
    Bibliography: p.
    I. Title.
PZ3.F7347Man3 [PT1863.S4]   833'.8   74-78439
ISBN 0-8044-2207-9
ISBN 0-8044-6155-4 (pbk.)

Introduction

1

"I asked him about his work. He was a don in Modern Languages, and he was writing a book about the German novelist Fontane." Thus the narrator in C. P. Snow's novel, *The Affair*. Even if he pleased not the multitude, Fontane never meant his books to be caviar to the general, and it is their loss if English-speaking countries are content to let him be the exclusive concern of specialists in Modern Languages as more of his masterly novels become available in translation. In Germany, west and east, Fontane has truly come into his own only since the war. The three excellent critical editions of his Works, the paperbacks of his fiction, the spate of discriminating studies, monographs, and bibliographical compilations bear eloquent testimony to it. This belated concentration of interest in an author who was preëminently the portraitist of Berlin society and the Brandenburg countryside may reflect the fact that the special status of Berlin since 1945 has meant, for

Germany, the absence of a capital as a social and cultural center as well as an administrative entity. It was in Fontane's day, notably after the proclamation of the Second German Reich early in 1871, that Berlin began to vie with London and Paris as a genuine metropolis.

What gives Fontane's novels their distinctive flavor is their poetic charm, their humor and gentle irony, their seemingly casual emphasis on minutiae, the *petits faits vrais*, that afford a glimpse behind the façade of the conversational poker game, above all their famous causerie and their Montaigne-like sanity and balance. Among Fontane's foremost admirers were Thomas and Heinrich Mann. Thomas Mann, who early acknowledged his debt to Fontane, wrote about him at length on several occasions throughout his life. His feelings for Fontane were summed up by Hermann Hesse in a letter after Mann's death and shortly before his own: "About Fontane, I never heard Thomas Mann speak with anything but downright tenderness."

Fontane's forebears on both sides were Huguenots from southern France who settled in Brandenburg, where the Great Elector had been quick to proclaim the "Edict of Potsdam" following Louis XIV's revocation of the Edict of Nantes in 1685. The family name was originally spelt Fontaine. Theodor Fontane, the son of an apothecary, was born in Neuruppin, near Berlin, in 1819, the same year as Melville, Whitman, Lowell, and George Eliot, and—auspiciously enough for a German writer whose association with mid-Victorian England was to have a profound influence on his life and work—

as Queen Victoria and the Prince Consort. In 1827, the family moved to the little town of Swinemünde on the Baltic where the older Fontane hoped to better his position with a newly acquired pharmacy. The five years in Swinemünde (the Kessin in Fontane's best-known novel, *Effi Briest*) form the core of the enchanting "autobiographical novel," as Fontane calls it, *Meine Kinderjahre* (*My Childhood Years*), written at his doctor's suggestion to surmount a severe depression that had threatened the completion of *Effi Briest*. In *Meine Kinderjahre*, through which Fontane in later years maintained he had recovered his health, the genial, happy-go-lucky figure of his father holds the center of the stage. The latter's "Socratic method" in the lessons he gave the boy at home, with their inexhaustible fund of anecdotal material from French history, laid the groundwork for Fontane's celebrated causerie and for his lifelong passion for history. There are indications of temperamental incompatibility between the parents (who eventually separated in 1850), which is reflected in the prominence the question of marriage assumes in Fontane's fiction.

The second autobiographical volume, *Von Zwanzig bis Dreissig* (*From Twenty to Thirty*), though less of a harmonious whole than the first, is full of vivid vignettes, with frequent shifts of the spotlight to both before and after the decade in question. But the emphasis is on this particular period, and we learn of Fontane's training and employment in pharmacy in Berlin, Leipzig, Dresden, of his growing absorption in literature, ballad writing, translating of English anti-Corn Law poets, his membership in the Berlin literary club *The Tunnel Over the Spree*, his military service and short leave for his first visit to England, his disappointment with the abortive Revolution of 1848, in which he briefly helped to man the barricades in Berlin; finally, of his exchange of pharmacy for journalism and of his marriage to his fiancée of five years' standing, Emilie (the same name as his mother's), who was also of French Huguenot extraction and as penniless as he. (Of the children of this marriage, three died in infancy; three sons and one daughter survived, including Friedrich, who became a publisher and in 1905–10 brought out a twenty-one volume edition of his father's Works.)

During a second, longer stay in England in 1852, Fontane explored the possibility of settling there, but nothing came of it. This was followed two years later by the publication of his first travel book, *Ein Sommer in London* (*A Summer in London*). Meanwhile, in Berlin, he had been put in charge of screening English newspapers at the Central Press Section of the Manteuffel Administration, which was increasingly at pains to justify its neutrality in the Crimean War. In September, 1855, the Press Section assigned him as its representative in London. He remained there until January, 1859, writing for a number of Prussian newspapers and periodicals on the political and above all cultural scene, which was closer to his heart, especially the theater and art exhibitions. His forte was reviewing Shakespearean productions on the London stage, often with Charles Kean in the leading role.

The years in England were to prove invaluable to Fontane in broadening his outlook and schooling his pen. His letters show him as a fascinated, but by no means uncritical, observer as Palmerstonian England, with the ascendancy of the commercial and industrial middle classes, hit her stride, much as Bismarckian Germany under Prussian leadership was to do in the seventies. He was an eager student of English and Scottish literature and history, and a visit to Scotland led to the publication (1860) of another travel book, *Jenseits des Tweed* (*Across the Tweed*), a forerunner of the series of volumes *Wanderungen durch die Mark Brandenburg* (*Journeys Through the Mark of Brandenburg*), which in turn were to pave the way for his fiction.

From 1860, until his resignation in 1870, Fontane worked as editor concerned with English affairs on the staff of the *Kreuzzeitung* in Berlin, with whose ultraconservative point of view he came to feel steadily more at odds. (This foreshadows his growing impatience in old age with outmoded diehard attitudes. Both in his last novel, *Der Stechlin* (*Lake Stechlin*), and in one of his late, plainspoken letters to an old doctor friend in London, he looked to the rise of the working class, the "fourth estate," as the only hope for social and political renewal.) A new departure for him during this period was a book on the Danish-Prussian war over Schleswig-Holstein in 1864 and another on Prussia's war with Austria in 1866, in which he draws on his visits to the respective theaters of operation. Later war books dealt with the Franco-Prussian war of 1870-71 and his experience as a war correspondent, including three months imprisonment by the French on a suspicion of espionage. (He never knew that he owed his release to Bismarck's personal intervention, with the American Minister in Paris serving as diplomatic channel.)

After deciding in 1870 to make his own way as a writer, Fontane contracted with the well-known *Vossische Zeitung* for regular coverage as its drama critic of productions at the Königliches Schauspielhaus. This provided not only an essential source of income but scope for continued critical writing. He wrote his reviews for the paper for nearly twenty years, starting with Schiller and ending with the young Gerhart Hauptmann, whom his column helped to launch.

Fontane's concern with the theater calls to mind his profound and lasting admiration for Shakespeare, to which an early tentative translation of *Hamlet*, first published in 1966, also bears witness. While he admired a host of other writers in world literature, Scott and Thackeray foremost among them, Shakespeare always headed the list. He was "a people's poet" ("*ein Volksdichter*"), who, seemingly content to entertain, was also a teacher and who showed us the "perfection of realism" by marrying realism and beauty and using humor as a means of transfiguring the attendant ugliness.

Having made his mark as a poet, primarily with his ballads, as a journalist, and as an author of war and travel books, Fontane was nearing sixty when he made his debut as a novelist with *Vor dem Sturm (Before the Storm)*, set in Prussia in the winter of 1812–13 as she prepares to shake off Napoleonic rule. During the next twenty years he kept writing and painstakingly revising, careful craftsman that he was, some seventeen novels in all, in addition to the two autobiographical volumes, drama criticism, and a voluminous correspondence, much of which has been published as constituting an integral part of his *oeuvre*. The phenomenon speaks for itself. Hawthorne, whose years as consul in Liverpool overlapped with Fontane's as foreign correspondent in London, had only strength and time enough left at that age for his travel book on England. Fontane had the good fortune to complete and revise his last novel before he died, between its serial and book publication, at his home in Berlin in 1898, three months short of seventy-nine.

II

"A small historical masterpiece [which] reveals the true and mature Fontane," says the noted late literary critic Georg Lukács of *Schach von Wuthenow*, the title of this novel in German. The idea of the novel was suggested to Fontane by an episode that he first learned about from an old friend and literary confidante, a Fräulein von Rohr, many years before most of the first draft came to be written in 1878. After completing two other novels in progress, Fontane returned to the present one in 1882. It was serialized in the *Vossische Zeitung* in Berlin in the summer and published in book form at Christmas of the same year (dated 1883), his fifth to appear. It has recently been translated into Japanese.

The anecdotal version underwent major transformations at Fontane's hands, including an important change of date from 1815 to the eve of Prussia's defeat by Napoleon at Jena and Auerstädt (October 14, 1806). This enabled Fontane to depict the climate in a Prussia gone to seed (Mirabeau's *pourriture* on page 4 as a portent of military defeat ("Hannibal *ante portas*" on page 15.) His choice of the ominous pre-Jena period in preference to the later date of the original episode was reinforced by his misgivings at the trends in his own day, especially since the victory over the French in the war of 1870–71.

The characters are made to speak for themselves without any moralizing intrusions on the author's part. The action centers on a cavalry officer in the elite Gensdarmes Regiment, Captain Schach von Wuthenow, who is in many ways symptomatic of Prussia in her decline, much as the very differently constituted romantic Jay Gatsby can be seen to epitomize Scott Fitzgerald's Jazz Age America. Schach's equivocal relationship with the attractive and socially ambitious Frau von Carayon and her pockmarked and self-effacing daughter Victoire is bedevilled by his morbid sensitivity to ridicule. "The fear of ridicule," says Fontane in a letter to his wife in connection with this novel, "is a function of tremendous importance in the world." It is Schach's Achilles heel and of a piece with his conformity to a society in which consideration of values is complacently subordinated to preservation of outward appearances. An officer cast in this mold is apt to look for a consort who could pass muster as a lady of style and beauty; a disfigured Victoire would compromise one's standing, however superior her hidden merits may be. And when one's entanglement raises the specter of a shotgun marriage, the dilemma is acute indeed.

Schach's excessive regard for outward appearances is in line with the absence of a first name for him. As in the case of Potiphar's wife, we are never told what it is. By withholding it Fontane reinforces the ceremonial stiffness that predominantly characterizes Schach's manner, his *persona*, over and above the air of formality we would expect at the military and social functions of the period. Even in his relationship with Victoire, it is only on the two occasions when she becomes his "Mirabelle" that he sufficiently unbends to shed entirely the impersonal rigidity we come to associate with the monosyllabic, guttural impact of his name. It is his epithet, his hallmark, and somehow places him equally as an individual and as a symbolic figure. At the same time, his surname (adapted from his prototype's Schack) is ironically suggestive, *Schach* being the German both for "chess" and for the move exposing the king to attack, "check." Its derivation from the Persian *shah* is skilfully exploited in the progressively devastating effect a series of cartoons is shown to have on their immediate target. The resort to ridicule, with a sharp edge of malice, represents the very opposite of what Fontane, in his letters and elsewhere, consistently advocates as one of the most estimable qualities in human relations: kindliness, decency, friendly disposition (*Wohlwollen*), a quality he regards as notoriously rare among advisers at the highest level of government when he makes a point of crediting the King's old aide-de-camp, Köckritz, with it.

For all his conventionalism, which extends to the political views he airs in debate, there is another, if submerged, side to Schach that makes him a more complex figure than he appears to those who try to get the better of him. He is in some respects an outsider and at times exhibits an inner loneliness (especially during his retreat on his estate), a secret longing for a spiritual goal (the symbolic Knight Templar), resentment of autocratic and paternalistic treatment (by the King and Queen and partly by Frau von Carayon), and a holding aloof from too close personal relations in general. This suggests an asymmetry which in its more pronounced and often pathological manifestation has come to be associated with the unheroic bourgeois hero in modern fiction. Schach is too tied to, too much a product of, the narrow and shallow code of his crumbling environment to transcend his limitations by attempting either a constructive breaking away or a balanced integration. An opportunity for the latter alternative is missed when at a crucial moment he fails to pay heed to what is perhaps the most authentic part of his nature beneath the drawing-room veneer, his religious stirrings. It is worth noting that he and Victoire are shown to be temperamentally most closely in accord in their discussion of the Templars.

In the first of the autobiographical volumes, *Meine Kinderjahre* (*Years of My Childhood*), Fontane warmly remembers the family's pockmarked housekeeper in Swinemünde, whose steadfast character had a formative influence on him. This recollection is clearly reflected in the portrayal of Victoire, outwardly disfigured and inwardly chastened by the effects of illness at an early age, attributes that mark her off from her mother. The mother-daughter motif, with which Schach's destiny is inextricably bound up, is sounded in the opening chapter even before he makes his first entrance: one can still tell that "her delicate profile must have resembled her mother's at one time." Schach, it is important to bear in mind, is a contemporary of Frau von Carayon's, as Innstetten is of the mother of Effi Briest.

A word should be said about Fontane's restraint in dealing with scenes of physical intimacy. He was no prude, but in his novels details we take for granted in fiction today are left to the reader's imagination with a delicacy of touch remarkable even by the canons of his time. Like all Fontane's fiction, the novel is full of spirited and yet finely shaded dialogue. Occasionally, as when Schach is lost in reverie, there are soliloquies on the stream-of-consciousness pattern, but they are used sparingly. And while the novel's concern is serious enough, humor and gentle irony help to keep the pervading tone safely pitched this side of tragedy. A subsidiary character like Victoire's superstitious Aunt Marguerite and such minor figures as Schach's English groom and his orderly Baarsch contribute their share to this end. Even when artistic beauty is invoked, as in the case of Dussek's musical swan flotilla, it is with a humorous touch. Correspondingly playful, and all the more effective for it, is the device of having the Roman emperor statues in the palace grounds in Charlottenburg wink at Schach, which enables us to infer from the projection of guilt his state of mind after he has been read the riot act by the King and told to give ear to the Queen. We are given an equally revealing clue when Schach, listening to Frau von Carayon's final summing up, lets the coffee drip in a slow trickle from his spoon— which anticipates "I have measured out my life with coffee spoons" in Eliot's "Prufrock."

The two letters comprising the epilogue have been critized as clumsy, somewhat contradictory, and too subjective in their comments. In a broader perspective, this cricism seems unjustified, however one responds to a particular literary convention. The letters complement each other and enhance the novel's intellectual and emotional resonance. They can be viewed in part as a sequel to some of the conversations, but the writers' tone is more reflective, more detached, but still sufficiently distinctive to suggest the degree of change undergone by each. The church in Rome mentioned by Victoire, Ara Cœli, is also noted by Henry Adams in the *Education* as the site where he, and Gibbon before him, had sat and mused. There, too, if in a different fashion, mystery and history converge. Implicit in Victoire's affirmation of love are the old Christian virtues of faith, hope, and charity. Noncommittal as Fontane was in his attitude to religion, it is significant that he decided to end on this note.

I should like to express my appreciation to Frederick Ungar for providing a forum for this work by a writer of the first rank who is still too little known in English-speaking countries.

This translation is dedicated with love and gratitude to my wife Margaret.

E.M.V.

London, 1974

I

In Frau von Carayon's Drawing Room

In the drawing room of Frau von Carayon and her daughter Victoire in the Behrenstrasse, a few friends were gathered at their hostess's usual soirée, though only a few, since the intense heat of the day had drawn even the most loyal habitués of the salon into the open air. Of the officers of the Gensdarmes Cavalry Regiment, who were rarely absent on any of these evenings, only one had appeared, a Herr von Alvensleben. He had seated himself beside the handsome lady of the house with a jocular expression of regret that the *very* person should be missing who was really entitled to this seat.

Seated opposite them both, on the side of the table facing the middle of the room, were two gentlemen in civilian clothes, who, though they had been frequenting this circle for only a few weeks, had none the less come to achieve a dominant position in it. Most markedly so the one who was by several years the younger of the two, a former staff captain, who since returning to his native soil after a checkered career in England and the United States was generally regarded as the leader of those military *frondeurs*[1] who were the inspiration, or rather terror, of the prevailing political opinion in the capital at that time. His name was von Bülow.[2] Nonchalance being one of the attributes of genius, he sat with both feet stretched far out in front, his left hand in his trouser pocket, his right hand sawing the air so as by lively gesticulations to lend emphasis to his sermon. He could, as his friends maintained, talk only to deliver a lecture, and he did indeed talk all the time. The stout gentleman beside him was the publisher of his writings, Herr Daniel Sander, but apart from this his exact opposite, at any rate as far as outward appearance was concerned. His face, framed by a black beard, revealed as much complacency as sarcasm, while a jacket made of holland cloth and narrowly fitted in the waist tightly laced up his *embonpoint*. What made the contrast between them complete was the exquisite white linen in which Bülow anything but excelled.

The conversation in which they were engaged seemed to concern the Haugwitz[3] delegation, which had just completed its mission and which in Bülow's view had not only led to a desirable restoration of harmonious relations between Prussia and France but had, in addition, secured Hanover for his countrymen by way of a "postnuptial gift."[4] Frau von Carayon, however, took exception to this "postnuptial gift," since one could not very well dispose of or make a present of something one did not possess, a remark that prompted her daughter Victoire, who had been busying herself unnoticed at the tea table until then, to fling her mother an affectionate glance, and Alvensleben to kiss the charming lady's hand.

"I was sure, dear Alvensleben," Frau von Carayon declared, "that you would agree with me. But look with what a Rhadamanthine and Minos-like air our friend Bülow is sitting there. It's the lull before the storm again with him. Victoire, do pass Herr von Bülow the Carlsbad wafers. It's the only thing Austrian, I expect, he'll tolerate. Meanwhile Herr Sander will tell us about the progress we're making in the new province. Only, it's none too impressive, I'm afraid."

"Nonexistent rather," Sander replied. "All those who identify with the Guelphic lion or the horse rampant of Brunswick have no stomach for Prussian tutelage. And I don't blame anyone for feeling like that. We may have been equal to dealing with the Poles perhaps, but the Hanoverians are a fastidious breed."

"Yes, so they are," Frau von Carayon acknowledged but was quick to add: "Though perhaps a trifle arrogant as well."

"A trifle!" Bülow laughed. "Oh, my dear madam, if everyone could always be let off as lightly as this! Believe me, I've known the Hanoverians for a good long time. As a native son of the Mark, I've been peeping over their fence, as it were, since I was a boy and so can assure you that everything that makes me loathe England can be found twice over in that ancestral land of the Guelphs I won't grudge them the benefit of the rod to which we're going to expose them. The mess we Prussians have made of things cries to high heaven, and Mirabeau was right when he compared the vaunted state of Frederick the Great to a fruit that had gone rotten before it was ripe. But rotten or not, there's *one* thing at least we can claim: an awareness that the world has taken a step forward these past fifteen years and that the great events of its destiny won't necessarily take place between the Nuthe and Notte.[5] But in Hanover they still think that Kalenberg[6] and Lüneburg Heath have a special mission to fulfill. *Nomen et omen.* It's the seat of stagnation, a hotbed of prejudice. At least *we* know that we're in a bad way, and this recognition contains the seeds of improvement. In matters of detail we may lag behind them, granted, but taken as a whole we're more advanced than they, and this entails rights and demands which we must assert. That our performance in Poland, Sander notwithstanding, was essentially a failure proves nothing. The government made no real effort and thought its tax collectors were perfectly good enough for spreading the blessings of civilization in the east. Justly so, to the extent that even a tax collector represents law and order, though the disagreeable side of it of course."

Victoire, who from the moment that Poland had been dragged into the conversation had left her place at the table, shook a warning finger at the speaker, saying:

"I want you to know, Herr von Bülow, that I love the Poles and, what's more, *de tout mon cœur.*"

And saying this, she leaned forward to emerge from the dark into the light of the lamp so that in its bright illumination one could clearly make out that her delicate profile must have resembled her mother's at one time but that it had been robbed of its former beauty by numerous pockmarks. Nobody could help seeing it, and the only one who did *not* see it or, if he did, regarded it as utterly immaterial, was Bülow. He merely repeated:

"Ah yes, the Poles. They dance the mazurka like nobody else. That's why you love them."

"Not at all. I love them because they are gallant and unfortunate."

"Fair enough. One can put it like that. And one might almost envy them for their misfortune, since it gains them the sympathy of every woman's heart. In the conquest of women their war record, from time immemorial, has been the most brilliant of all."

"And who was it who liberated . . ."

"You know my heretical views about liberations. And Vienna of all places![7] It was liberated, certainly. But to what purpose? My imagination fairly runs riot at the thought of some favorite sultana standing in the crypt of the Capuchins, perhaps at the very spot where Maria Theresa stands now. A vestige of Islam has always been well ingrained in these cock-and-pheasant gluttons, and Europe could have put up with a little more of the seraglio or harem business without being greatly the worse for it . . ."

A servant came in to announce Cavalry Captain von Schach, and both women fleetingly betrayed a flicker of happy surprise as the newly announced guest presently entered the room. He kissed Frau von Carayon's hand, bowed to Victoire, and greeted Alvensleben in a cordial manner but Bülow and Sander with reserve.

"I fear I have interrupted Herr von Bülow . . ."

"Inevitably so, indeed," Sander replied, moving his chair aside.

Everybody laughed, Bülow himself joined in, and only Schach's more than usual reserve suggested that in entering the drawing room he must have been under the effect of either some disagreeable personal experience or a politically unpleasant piece of news.

"What news have you, dear Schach? You look distrait. Have any new disasters. . . ?"

"It's not *that*, madam, not that. I'm coming from Countess Haugwitz, on whom I call all the more frequently the further I find myself removed from the Count and his policy. The Countess knows it and approves of my conduct. We had barely begun our conversation when a mob began to collect in front of the palace, hundreds at first, then thousands. All the time the uproar kept mounting, and in the end someone threw a stone that whizzed past the table at which we were sitting. A hairsbreadth, and the Countess would have been hit. But what *did* hit her hard was the shouting, the abuse resounding from the street. Eventually, the Count himself appeared. He had himself completely under control and never for a moment belied the gentleman. However, it was a long time before the street could be cleared. Is this what we've come to then— riots, disorders? And that in the state of Prussia, under His Majesty's[8] very eyes."

"And it's especially on *us*, especially on us of the Gensdarmes Regiment," Alvensleben interposed, "that responsibility for these incidents will be heaped. They know we frown on all this toadying to France, from which we have ultimately nothing to gain but some stolen provinces. Everybody knows where we stand in this matter, at court, too, they know, and they won't hesitate to put the onus for this tumult on *us*."

"A sight for the gods," said Sander. "The Gensdarmes Regiment in the dock for high treason and disturbance of the peace."

"And not unjustly," Bülow, now genuinely agitated, broke in. "Not unjustly, I say. And your quips aren't going to dispose of that, Sander. Why do the gentlemen who day in and day out profess to know everything better than the King and his ministers, why do they take this line? Why do they politicize? Whether soldiers are free to politicize is an open question, but if they *must* politicize, let them at least politicize in accordance with the facts. At long last we're on the right track, at long last we've reached the point where we should have been in the first place, at long last His Majesty has listened to the voice of reason. And what happens? Our gentlemen officers, whose every other word is of the King and their loyalty and who always feel in their element only when there's a scent of Russia and Russia leather in the air, and precious little of freedom, our gentlemen officers, I say, all of a sudden yield to a taste for opposition as naive as it is dangerous and by their arrogant behavior and still more arrogant pronouncements provoke the anger of the barely placated imperator.[9] It's the sort of thing that quickly takes root in the street. The gentlemen of the Gensdarmes Regiment will not of course themselves pick up the stone that's destined to land near the Countess's tea table, but they're the moral instigators of the disturbance none the less, *they* having prepared the mental climate for it."

"No, the climate was there."

"All right. Perhaps it was. But *if* it was, what was needed was to fight, not to fan, it. By fanning it we hasten our doom. The Emperor[9] is only waiting for an opportunity, with plenty of charges in his ledger against our account, and once he adds up the total, we'll be done for."

"I don't think so," retorted Schach. "I can't go along with you there, Herr von Bülow."

"Which I regret."

"I can't say I do. It's easy enough for you to be generous with advice and guidance to my brother officers and me about loyalty to King and country: after all, the principles you espouse happen to be the order of the day. We're now, as you would wish and as laid down at the highest level, standing at France's table, gathering up the crumbs that are falling off the Emperor's table. But for how long? It's time that the state of Frederick the Great remembered what it owes to itself."

"If only it would," Bülow replied. "But that's just what it neglects to do. Is this vacillating, this lingering flirtation with Russia and Austria, which has alienated the *empereur*[9] from us, *is* this in the tradition of Frederickian foreign policy? I ask you."

"You misunderstand me."

"Then I'd be obliged if you would deliver me of this misunderstanding."

"I'll try to at least . . . Incidentally, you're *bent* on misunderstanding me, Herr von Bülow. I'm opposed to the French alliance not because it is an alliance, nor because, in the nature of all alliances, it is meant for the sake of this or that particular objective to double our strength. Oh, no, how could I? Alliances are indispensable devices for *every* foreign policy: even the great King[10] made use of such devices and within the framework of such devices was always *flexible*. But where he was *not* flexible was in the pursuit of his ultimate goal. That remained fixed: a strong and independent Prussia. And now I ask you, Herr von Bülow, is *that* what Count Haugwitz has brought back for us, and of which you so highly approve, is *that* a strong and independent Prussia? You've asked *me*; now I'm asking *you*."

II

The Consecration of Strength

Bülow, who showed signs of assuming an air of extreme hauteur, was about to reply, but Frau von Carayon intervened, saying:

"Let's profit by the example of the current international scene: where peace proves elusive, let there at least be a truce. Here too . . . And now, dear Alvensleben, guess who came to pay us a visit today. A person of prominence. And sent to us by Rahel Levin."[1]

"Well, then, the Prince,"[2] Alvensleben said.

"Ah, no, more prominent, or at any rate more prominently in the news. The Prince is a well-established celebrity and those who have been celebrities for ten years have ceased to be any . . . Anyhow, I'll give you a clue: it inclines toward the literary, and now I feel sure Herr Sander is going to solve the problem for us."

"At least I'll try to, madam, in which your confidence may perhaps lend me a certain consecratory strength or, to come right out with it, a certain *Consecration of Strength*."³

"Oh, splendid. Yes, it was Zacharias Werner who called. Unfortunately, we were out so that we were deprived of the pleasure of his intended visit. I was so sorry."

"You should, on the contrary, consider yourself fortunate to have been spared a disillusionment," Bülow began. "It's rare for poets to measure up to the image we've formed of them. We expect to see an Olympian, a nectar-and-ambrosia man, and behold instead a gourmand eating roast turkey. We expect to learn about his most intimate communion with the gods and hear him hold forth about his latest decoration or even recite the ever so gracious pronouncements of His Serene Highness about the most recent offspring of his muse, or perhaps of *Her* Serene Highness, something that always represents the last word in fatuousness."

"Still, no more fatuous than the opinions of those privileged to have been born in a stable or barn," Schach remarked caustically.

"I regret, my dear Herr von Schach, to have to disagree with you in *this* area as well. The distinction you dispute is, in *my* experience at least, an established fact, one, moreover, as you will allow me to repeat, that argues *not* in favor of His Serene Highness. In the world of the man in street, critical opinion as such is not superior, but the guise of self-conscious diffidence it assumes and the hemming and hawing bad faith with which it is conveyed always produce something of a disarming effect. And now the Sovereign makes himself heard! His voice is the law of the land in every conceivable sphere, in matters great and small, hence in aesthetics of course as well. He who passes on issues of life and death, shouldn't he be competent to pass on the merits of a little poem too? Oh, bah! No matter what his pronouncements may be, they're always the tables straight from the Mount. I've listened to the proclamation of such a decalogue more than once and come to appreciate since what is meant by *regarder dans le néant.*"[4]

"And yet I agree with Mama," said Victoire, anxious to guide the conversation back to the original point, that is, to the play and the dramatist. "I really would have enjoyed meeting the gentleman 'prominently in the news,' to use Mama's qualifying description of him. You forget, Herr von Bülow, that we're *women* and as such may invoke the privilege of curiosity. To find little to admire in a person of prominence is after all preferable to never having laid eyes on him at all."

"And we certainly shan't go to see him now," Frau von Carayon added. "He'll be leaving Berlin within the next few days, and anyway, he'd only come to attend the first rehearsals of his play."

"In other words," Alvensleben broke in, "the production itself is no longer in doubt."

"No, I don't think it is. They've succeeded in persuading the Court to agree, or at any rate in disposing of all the misgivings that had been voiced."

"Which is beyond me," Alvensleben went on. "I've read the play. He is at pains to present Luther in an exalted light, and at every turn the cloven hoof of Jesuitism keeps peeping below the hem of the doctoral gown. But to me the greatest puzzle of all is that Iffland[5] should feel drawn to it, Iffland, a Freemason."

"From which I would simply conclude that he has the leading role," Sander replied. "Our principles remain in force just as long as they don't clash with our passions and conceits, when they invariably get the worst of it. Clearly, his heart is set on acting Luther, and that settles it."

"I confess I dislike seeing the figure of Luther put on the stage," said Victoire. "Or am I going too far in this?"

It was Alvensleben to whom the question had been addressed.

"Oh, my dearest Victoire, of course not. You've expressed exactly my own feelings. My earliest memories are sitting in our village church and my old father beside me joining in the singing of every verse from the hymnbook. And to the left of the altar, there was our Martin Luther in a full-length portrait on the wall, the Bible cradled in his arm, his right hand placed on top, a picture throbbing with life, and looking across at me. I may say that on many a Sunday those sedate, manly features would preach more effectively and movingly to me than that clucking old hen of ours who, true enough, had the same high cheekbones and the same white bands as the Reformer, but nothing else. And this godly man, from whom we derive our denomination and distinctive identity, to whom I've never looked up with anything but reverence and devotion, he isn't one I'd like to see emerge from the wings or a backdoor of the stage. Not even if Iffland is playing the part for whom, incidentally, I have a high regard, not only as an artist but also as a man of principle and solid Prussian heart."

"*Pectus facit oratorem,*"[6] Sander affirmed, seconded by Victoire's exclamation of delight.

But Bülow, who did not take kindly to new rival gods, flung himself back in his chair, saying as he stroked his chin and goatee:

"It won't surprise you to see me registering dissent."

"Heavens no," Sander laughed.

"All I want to guard against is that my dissent is taken to mean that I'm pleading the cause of that popish Zacharias Werner whom with his fondness for the mystical-romantic I simply detest. I'm not pleading anyone's cause . . ."

"Not even Luther's?" Schach asked ironically.

"Not even Luther's!"

"What a good thing he can afford to do without it . . ."

"But for how long?" Bülow, sitting up, continued. "Believe me, Herr von Schach, *he* too is caught up in the prevailing decadence like so much else beside him, and before long no general pleading of causes in the world will be able to prop him up."

"I have heard Napoleon speak of a 'Prussia episode,' " retorted Schach. "Are the gentlemen of the new school, and Herr von Bülow foremost among them, perhaps going to treat us to a 'Luther episode' as well?"

"Just so. You've put your finger on it. It's not *our* doing, by the way, this episode business. That sort of thing is not the doing of the individual but of history. And at the same time a remarkable correlation between

the Prussia and Luther episodes will be seen to exist.
Here too the motto is: 'Tell me whose company you
keep and I will tell you who you are.' I admit I think the
days of Prussia are numbered, and 'when the purple
drops the Duke must follow suit.'[7] The dramatis per-
sonae involved I leave to you to work out. The correla-
tions between state and church are not sufficiently appreciated; every state is in a certain sense implicitly also
an *ecclesiastical state*; it enters into marriage with the
church, and if the marriage is to be a happy one, the two
will have to be well matched. In Prussia, they are well
matched. And why? Because they are both equally in-
adequate by nature, have proved equally narrow in
scope. They're parochial entities, both destined to be
encompassed or absorbed by some larger framework.
And soon in fact. Hannibal *ante portas*."[8]

"What I understand you to be saying," Schach replied, "is that Count Haugwitz has brought us not our
doom, but salvation and peace."

"Yes, he has. But he can't change our destiny, not in
the long run at least. That destiny means integration
into the universal. The national and denominational per-
spectives are dying phenomena, especially the Prussian
perspective and its *alter ego*, the Lutheran. Both are
artificial dimensions. What do they amount to, I wonder, what purpose do they serve? They draw on the
assets of each other's accounts, reciprocally agents of
need and demand, and that's as far as it goes. And this is
supposed to be acting on the scale of a world power?
What has Prussia done for the good of the world?

What's the sum total I arrive at when I add it all up?
The tall regimentals in blue of Frederick William I, the
iron ramrod, the pigtail, and that magnificent ethos that
coined the phrase: 'I tied him to the crib, why wouldn't
he eat?' "⁹

"Granted, granted. But Luther ..."

"Very well then. There's a myth abroad to the effect
that the advent of the gentleman of Wittenberg marked
the birth of freedom in the world, and hidebound his-
torians have dinned this into the ears of the people of
North Germany until they've come to believe it. But
what did he really bequeath to the world? Intolerance
and witchhunts, lack of imagination and boredom. Not
the kind of cement to weather the millennia of the ages.
That universal monarchy which requires only the finish-
ing touch will also call forth a universal religion. For
just as small things sort themselves out and exhibit their
interdependence, so do the big ones, even far more
conspicuously. I have no intention of seeing the Luther
that's being put on the stage, because in the distorted
version of Herr Zacharias Werner it's just something
that happens to annoy me, but to refuse to see it because
it would give offense, because it would be a *profanation*,
that's beyond my comprehension."

"And we, dear Bülow," Frau von Carayon interrupted,
"we're going to see him, despite the fact that it will give
us offense. Victoire is right, and if in Iffland's case vanity
may be said to get the better of principle, in *ours* it's
curiosity. I hope Herr von Schach and you, dear Alvensleben, will join us. By the way, some of the inter-

polated songs are not at all bad. Victoire, you might sing one or two of them for us."

"I've barely been through them on the piano yet."

"Oh, in that case I'd appreciate it all the more," said Schach. "I hate all displays of drawing-room virtuosity. What does appeal to me in art is a kind of poetic searching and groping."

Bülow smiled to himself as if to say: "Everyone after his own fashion."

Schach meanwhile led Victoire to the piano, and she sang as he accompanied her:

> *Die Blüte, sie schläft so leis und lind*
> *Wohl in der Wiege von Schnee;*
> *Einlullt sie der Winter: "Schlaf ein, geschwind,*
> *Du blühendes Kind."*
> *Und das Kind, es weint und verschläft sein Weh,*
> *Und hernieder steigen aus duftiger Höh*
> *Die Schwestern und lieben und blühn . . .* *

There was a brief pause, and Frau von Carayon asked:

"Well, Herr Sander, what comment does this invite from you?"

"I'm sure it's very beautiful," he replied. "I don't understand it. But let's listen to the rest. The blossom that's still asleep is bound to wake up at some point."

---

* The blossom is so peacefully and gently asleep in the cradle of snow no doubt; winter's lullaby rocks it to sleep: "Quick, go to sleep, you blossomy child." And the child, it cries and buries its anguish in sleep. And from the misty heavens its sisters descend, full of love and in bloom.

Und kommt der Mai dann wieder so lind,
Dann bricht er die Wiege von Schnee,
Er schüttelt die Blüte: "Wach auf geschwind,
Du welkendes Kind."
Und es hebt die Äuglein, es tut ihm weh,
Und steigt hinauf in die leuchtende Höh,
Wo strahlend die Brüderlein blühn.*

There was no lack of vigorous applause, but it was meant exclusively for Victoire and the composition, and when they finally also turned to the text, they all echoed Sander's heretical views.

Only Bülow was silent. Like most *frondeurs* occupied with the decline and fall of the state, he had his soft spots, too, and one of them had been affected by the song. A few stars were twinkling in the partly overcast sky outside, and set between them was the crescent of the moon. Looking up through the panes of the high balcony door, he repeated:

"Wo strahlend die Brüderlein blühn."

Willy-nilly and without being aware of it, he was a child of his age and yielding to a sentimental mood.

They sang a second and a third song, but their opinion remained the same. Then they broke up at a not too unreasonable hour.

---

* And May upon its gentle return bursts the cradle of snow. It shakes the blossom: "Quickly, awake, you child that's fading away." And it opens its eyes, is gripped by pain, and ascends to the heavens aglow with the radiance of its little brothers that are in bloom.

III

At Sala Tarone's

The clock towers in Gensdarmes Square were striking eleven when Frau von Carayon's guests came out into the Behrenstrasse and, turning left, walked in the direction of the Linden. The moon was now veiled in clouds and the humidity which already permeated the air and foreshadowed a break in the weather was welcomed by all with a sense of relief. At the corner of the Linden, Schach, under pretext of various official commitments, took his leave, while Alvensleben, Bülow, and Sander decided on another hour's chat.

"But where?" Bülow asked, who, though on the whole not particular in his choice, nevertheless disliked places where "manager and waiter made him choke."

"But where?" Sander echoed. "Look, fortune lies on your doorstep,"[1] and he pointed to a corner establishment above which a sign in medium-sized characters announced: Sala Tarone's Italian Wine & Delicatessen Restaurant. Since it was past closing time, they knocked

at the front door, which was fitted with a covered aper-
ture on one side. And indeed, it was presently opened
from the inside, a head appeared at the peephole, and
when Alvensleben's uniform had provided reassurance
about the nature of the somewhat late clientele, the key
in the door lock on the other side was turned and the
three of them trooped in. But a draft that was blowing
put out the candle in the reflector-backed candlestick
the cellarer was holding in his hand, and the guttering
light of a lantern in the far rear immediately above the
courtyard entrance was only just bright enough to reveal the hazards obstructing the passageway.

"Look here, Bülow, how d'you like this defile?"
Sander growled, pulling in his stomach inch by inch,
and one certainly had to be careful, since in front of the
oil and wine barrels on either side there were lemon and
orange crates, their tops raised up towards the aisle.

"Watch your step," said the cellarer. "There are tacks
and nails all over the place. Ran one into my foot only
yesterday."

"And chevaux-de-frise, too . . . Oh, Bülow, a military
publisher would land one in a situation like this."

This moan of Sander's restored the cheerful tone and,
stumbling and groping, they finally found themselves
near the courtyard entrance where, towards the right,
some of the barrels were not lying quite so close together. Here they managed to squeeze through and
using a steep flight of four or five steps, reached a back
room of medium size, its yellow paint almost black with
smoke which, after the fashion of all "breakfast rooms,"

was most crowded at midnight. Everywhere, along the wainscoting, stood long leather sofas with well-worn seats, small and big tables in front of them, and there was only *one* place where this type of furniture was not in evidence. Here, instead, there was a desk surmounted by a stack of boxes and shelves in front of which one of the restaurateurs would be perched day in and day out on a swivel stool, calling down his orders (usually confined to one word) to the cellar beside his desk through the trapdoor that was always open.

Our friends had seated themselves in a corner diagonally across from the cellar hatch and Sander, who had been a publisher just long enough to be conversant with Lucullan delicacies, was scanning the menu and wine list. It was bound in russia leather, but smelt of lobster. Our Lucullus, it seemed, had not found anything he fancied. He therefore pushed the menu away again, saying:

"The least I'd expect when reminded of the dog days in an April like this is some blossomy flavor of May, *asperula odorata Linnéi*.[2] After all, I've also published things on botany. That there's a supply of fresh oranges about we were able to see for ourselves out there at the risk of our necks, and for the Moselle we can depend on the house."

The gentleman at the desk did not stir, but he was plainly registering assent with his back, Bülow and Alvensleben followed suit, and Sander tersely settled it:

"Well, then, May wine."

The word was uttered in a deliberately loud tone and

with the insistence of a command, and then and there a voice from the swivel stool boomed out into the cave below:

"Fritz!"

With only the upper half of his body visible at first, a stocky, bullnecked boy presently shot up from the hatch as though released by a spring and, skipping in an eager show of duty the last two or three steps with one steadying hand, planted himself in a flash in front of Sander as the one he obviously knew best.

"Tell us, Fritz, how does the house of Sala Tarone feel about May wine?"

"Fine. First rate."

"But it's only April, and though I'm normally a great believer in artificial flavoring, there's one thing I hate: tonka beans. They belong in the snuff box, not in May wine. D'you follow me?"

"At your service, Herr Sander."

"All right. Natural herbs then. And not to be steeped too long. Woodruff is no camomile tea. The Moselle, say a Zeltinger or Brauneberger, slowly to be poured over the leaves. That'll do. A few slices of orange just for decoration. One too many brings on a headache. And not too sweet, and an extra bottle of Cliquot. An extra one, mind you. Safe is safe."

This completed the order, and before another ten minutes had passed, the punch was brought up, with only three or four leaves floating on top, just enough to attest to its genuineness.

"You see, Fritz, that's what I like. Often there's something like duckweed floating about in the punch. And that's disgusting. I think we'll remain friends. And now for some green glasses."

Alvensleben laughed. "Green ones?"

"Yes, I'm aware of the objections, dear Alvensleben, and accept them. In fact, it's a subject I've been pondering for some time and which, like some others, belongs to that category of anomalies which, no matter how we set about things, are persistent features of our life. The color of wine is dispensed with, but the color of spring comes into its own, thus bringing into play the whole panoply of the ritual color scheme. And this seems to me the overriding point. Our partaking of food and drink, to the extent that it doesn't serve the universal need of mere survival, is bound increasingly to represent a symbolic act, and I can make sense of those periods of the late Middle Ages when the centerpiece on the dining table and the fruit bowls would mean more than the meal itself."

"How admirably this suits you, Sander," Bülow laughed. "All the same, thank heavens I don't have to pay your capon bill."

"Which you're paying for *none the less*."

"Ah, the *first* time I detect an appreciative publisher in you. This calls for clinking glasses . . . But for goodness' sake, there's beanpole Nostitz coming up the hatch. Look at him, Sander, how tall can you get . . ."

True enough, it was Nostitz who, having used a secret entrance, was tripping up the cellar stairs, Nostitz,[3] of the Gensdarmes Regiment, the tallest lieutenant in the army. Though from Saxony, he had been assigned to that crack regiment because of his six feet three by and large without any open opposition, and had long since got the better of a slight lingering trace of resentment. A reckless horseman and an even more reckless lady's man and contractor of debts, he had long been a supremely popular figure in the Regiment, so popular that the "Prince"—meaning none other than Prince Louis—had at the time of mobilization the year before asked that he be made his adjutant.

Curious to learn where he had come from, they bombarded him with questions, but not until he had made himself comfortable on the leather sofa did he reply to their barrage.

"Where do I come from? Why did I play truant from the Carayons? Well, because I wanted to take a look at Französisch-Buchholz[4] to see whether the storks were back, whether the cuckoo has started to call again, and whether the schoolmaster's daughter still has those long flaxen-blond pigtails she had last year. A lovely child. I always make her show me over the church, and then we climb up to the belfry, because inscriptions on old bells are a passion with me. You have no idea what discoveries one can make in a tower like that. I count them among the happiest and most instructive hours I've spent."

"And a blonde, you said. That of course explains everything. After all, our Fräulein Victoire cannot hope to compete with a Princess Goldilocks. And not even her beautiful mama can, who is beautiful, though still a brunette. And blonde hair always wins out over black."

"I wouldn't exactly elevate this into an axiom," Nostitz resumed. "It really all depends on the surrounding circumstances, which in this case of course also argue in favor of my young friend. The beautiful mama, as you call her, is going on for thirty-seven, in the computation of which I trust I'm gentleman enough to be *halving* instead of *doubling* her four years of married life. But that's for Schach to worry about, who sooner or later will have a chance to explore the secrets of her baptismal certificate."

"How so?" Bülow asked.

"How so?" Nostitz returned. "How undiscerning scholars, even soldier-scholars, really are. You mean the relationship between those two has escaped your notice? One that's at a fairly advanced stage, I believe. *C'est le premier pas qui coûte* . . ."[5]

"You're rather beating about the bush, Nostitz."

"Not usually exactly one of my vices."

"For my part, I think I see what you're driving at," Alvensleben put in. "But you're mistaken, Nostitz, if you take this to imply a match. Schach's makeup is a very peculiar one, which, whatever fault one may find with it, certainly has its share of psychological problems. I've never for example met anyone with whom everything could be laid so exclusively to the aesthetic, which may perhaps be somehow bound up with the fact that he has exaggerated notions of integrity and marriage. At least of the kind of marriage *he* would like to contract. And therefore I'm as certain as I am that I breathe that he'd never marry a widow, not even the greatest beauty. But should there still be any doubt about this, there's *one* factor that would dispose of it, and that factor is called 'Victoire'."

"How so?"

"Just as many a matrimonial scheme has fallen through because of an unprepossessing mother, so it would in this instance be sure to fall through because of an unprepossessing daughter. He feels her marred beauty to be a downright embarrassment, and is horrified at the thought of seeing his normality, if I may put it like that, becoming in any way tied up with her abnormality. He's morbidly dependent—dependent to the point of helplessness—on what people think of him, especially those of his class, and would always feel it to be beyond him to introduce Victoire as his daughter to some princess or other or even only to a lady of the higher strata of society."

"Perhaps. But that sort of thing can be got around."

"Hardly. To relegate her to the background, or to treat her just like a Cinderella, that's contrary to his innate sense of tact. His heart's too much in the right spot for that. Nor would Frau von Carayon simply put up with it, since as surely as she's attached to Schach as surely is she attached to Victoire, in fact, her attachment to the latter goes a great deal *further*. Between mother and daughter there's an absolutely perfect relationship, and it's this relationship more than anything else that has made me and continues to make me cherish their house so much."

"All right, let's drop the match," said Bülow. "Personally, all the more gratifying and welcome to me, because I adore that woman. She has about her all the magic of the true and natural, and even her defects have a charm and appeal. And by contrast, this man *Schach*! He may have his qualities, for all I know, but to me he's just a pompous prig and at the same time the embodiment of that Prussian parochialism which operates with exactly three articles of faith: article one, 'the world rests no more securely on the shoulders of Atlas than the state of Prussia rests on the shoulders of the Prussian army'; article two, 'a Prussian infantry offensive defies resistance'; thirdly and lastly, 'no battle is ever lost so long as the Garde du Corps Regiment hasn't gone over to the attack.' Or also of course the Gensdarmes Regiment. After all, they're siblings, twin brothers. I loathe this kind of rhetoric, and the day isn't far off when the world will see through the sham of rodomontades like these."

"And yet you do underrate Schach. He's still one of our best men about."

"So much the worse."

"One of our best, I maintain, and *really* a decent sort. He doesn't just act the knight in shining armor, he truly *is* one. Of course, after his own fashion. Anyhow, he wears an honest face and no mask."

"Alvensleben is right," Nostitz agreed. "I don't much care for him, but it's true, everything about him is sincere, including the stiff formality of manner, dull and supercilious as I find it. And in *this* respect he's different from us. He's always himself, whether he's entering a drawing room or standing in front of a mirror, or putting on his saffron-colored overnight gloves when going to bed. Sander, who hasn't much use for him, shall pass judgment and have the final word about him."

"It's barely three days," the latter began, "that I read in Haude and Spener's *Berlin News* that the Emperor of Brazil had promoted St. Anthony to the rank of lieutenant-colonel and directed his minister of war to enter the pay to the credit of said saint until further notice. Which credit arrangement impressed me even more than did the promotion. But be that as it may. In times of such appointments and promotions it won't be thought extravagant if I sum up the sentiments of the present hour, as well as the verdict and sentence I've been asked to pronounce, by declaring: His Majesty Captain of the Cavalry von Schach, long may he live!"

"Oh, splendid, Sander," said Bülow, "you've hit the nail on the head. The whole ludicrous business in a nutshell. The little man in the big boots! But for all I care: long may he live!"

"Thus we wind up with the eloquence of 'His Majesty's Most Loyal Opposition' into the bargain," Sander countered, getting up. "And now, Fritz, the bill. If you'll allow me, gentlemen, I'll see to the necessaries."

"Couldn't be left in more capable hands," said Nostitz.

And five minutes later they all strode out into the street again. A swirl of dust was being blown up the Linden from the direction of Brandenburg Gate, a heavy thunderstorm was plainly imminent, and the first big drops were already beginning to fall.

"*Hâtez-vous.*"[6]

And they all heeded this advice in an effort to get home as quickly as possible and by the shortest route.

IV

At Tempelhof

The following morning found Frau von Carayon and her daughter in the same corner room in which they had been hosts to their friends the night before. Both of them were attached to the room and would single it out in preference to all the others. It had three tall windows; two that were placed at right angles to each other looked out on the Behren- and Charlottenstrasse, the third, in the manner of French doors, took up the entire round corner and opened on to a balcony which was enclosed by a gilt railing in rococo style. As soon as the season permitted, this balcony door would be left open so that from almost anywhere in the room one had a view of the activity in the neighboring streets which, despite the district's exclusiveness, was often an unusually lively one, especially at the time of the military spring parades. Then not only the Berlin garrison's famous old regiments but, what to the Carayons was more to the point, also the Garde du Corps and Gensdarmes Regiments would pass by their house to the sound of silver trumpets. On those occasions (when the eyes of the officers, needless to say, would be darting up to the balcony) the corner room really came into its own and could not have been exchanged for any of the others.

But the room was an attractive one on quiet days, too, elegant and cozy at the same time. Here lay the Oriental rug, relic of the brilliant Petersburg days nearly half a generation ago, here stood the malachite mantelpiece clock, a gift of Catherine the Great, and here above all the large, richly gilded piér glass was on display that would daily be called upon to reassure the beautiful lady that she was the beautiful lady still. Although Victoire never missed an opportunity for setting her mother's mind at rest on this vital point, Frau von Carayon was astute enough to have this confirmed every morning anew by scrutinizing her image in the mirror herself. Whether her glance at such moments would stray above the sofa to the full-length portrait, complete with red ribbon, of Herr von Carayon, or whether a more imposing likeness would take shape in her mind, was something about which no one even moderately familiar with the domestic state of affairs had any doubts. For Herr von Carayon had been a swarthy little Frenchman of the local French colony who, except for a few eminent Carayons in the environs of Bordeaux and his proud service on the Legation staff, had contributed nothing very remarkable to the union. Least of all manly good looks.

It was striking eleven, first outside, then in the corner

room where both ladies were engaged on an embroidery frame. The balcony door was wide open, since despite the rain which had lasted until morning there was again a bright sun in the sky, producing much the same kind of sultriness as had prevailed the day before. Victoire, looking up from her work, recognized Schach's little groom coming up Charlottenstrasse in top boots and a hat exhibiting two color bands which she was wont to refer to as Schach's "national colors."

"Oh, look," said Victoire, "there's Schach's little Ned. And what airs he's giving himself again. But then he's allowed his own way too much and is turning more and more into a doll. What's he coming for I wonder?"

She was not kept wondering long. A minute later they heard the doorbell ring, an old retainer in leggings, a survivor of the elegant Petersburg days, came in with a note on a small silver salver. Victoire picked it up. It was addressed to Frau von Carayon.

"For *you*, Mama."

"Go on, read it," she said.

"No, you do. I've an aversion to mysteries."

"Goose," her mother laughed, opening the note, and read:

Dear Madam:
The rain last night has helped to improve not only the roads but also the air. All in all, as fine a day as April only rarely grants us hyperboreans.[1] I propose to be in front of your house with my chaise at four o'clock to collect you and Fräulein Victoire for a drive. As for the destination, I await

your instructions. You realize, don't you, the pleasure it gives me to be allowed to comply with your commands. Kindly send me word by the messenger. He is just sufficiently fluent in German not to get a *Ja* and *Nein* mixed up. Regards and remembrances to my good friend Victoire (who, to be on the safe side, could perhaps write a line).

Yours,
Schach

"Well, Victoire, what message do we send back . . . ?"
"But, surely, you can't be asking seriously, Mama."
"Well then, it's 'yes'."
Victoire had meanwhile sat down at her writing desk and her pen was scribbling away:

Most delighted to accept, even though the destination is as yet obscure. But once the crucial moment is at hand, it will no doubt let us make the right choice.

Frau von Carayon was reading over Victoire's shoulder.
"It sounds so ambiguous," she said.
"Then I'll simply write 'yes' and you countersign."
"No, just leave it."
And Victoire sealed the note and handed it to the groom, who was waiting outside.
As she reentered the room from the corridor, she found her mother in a pensive mood.
"I don't care for such piquancies, and least of all for such cryptic phrases."
"But then, *you* couldn't afford to write them. Whereas

I? I've a completely free hand. And now look here. Something's got to be done, Mama. People keep talking so, even to me, and since Schach still maintains silence and you can't *afford* to speak up, I'll have to do it for both of you and arrange a match. There always comes a time in life when roles are reversed. Normally, mothers marry off their daughters, in this instance the situation is different, and I marry you off. He loves you and you love him. You're the same age and are going to be the most handsome couple that's been led to the altar in the French Cathedral or at Trinity Church within living memory. You see, at least I give you full freedom of choice regarding the clergyman and church. Beyond that I can't go in this matter. That you enter this union saddled with me is no advantage, but no calamity either. Where there's much light there's deep shade."

Frau von Carayon's eyes filled with tears.

"Oh, Victoire, my sweet, you see it differently from the way it is. I don't want to stagger you with any confessions, and merely dropping veiled hints, as you're sometimes fond of doing, goes against the grain. Nor do I want to philosophize. But *one* thing you may be sure of, everything is preordained in us, and what seems to be cause is for the most part just as much effect and consequence. Believe me, your little hand is *not* going to tie the knot that you're thinking of tying. It's not in the cards, it can't be done. I'm a better judge of it. And besides, what would be the point? When all is said and done, I really love no one but *you*."

Their conversation was interrupted by the arrival of

an old lady, a sister of the late Herr von Carayon, who on Tuesdays was invariably invited to their midday meal and who with punctual habit would interpret "to the midday meal" to mean twelve o'clock, even though she knew they did not serve at the Carayons' until three. Aunt Marguerite, which was her name, was a true surviving specimen of the ladies of the French colony. In other words, an old lady who spoke the Berlin vernacular of the period, its inflection almost entirely confined to the dative, with rounded, thrust-out lips, preferring the French "u" to the German "i," so that the cherries she ate would be *Kürschen* rather than *Kirschen* and the church she attended a *Kürche* rather than a *Kirche*, and embellishing her speech, needless to say, with French locutions and forms of address. Neat and old-fashioned in her dress, she would summer and winter alike wear the same short silk overcoat. And she had that slightly humpbacked figure which was so common among the old ladies of the colony that Victoire when still a child had once asked, "How is it, Mama dear, that nearly all the aunts are so 'what d'you call it?'" and by way of illustration had hunched up one shoulder. Aunt Marguerite's silk overcoat was matched by a pair of silk gloves by which she set particularly great store, always waiting to put them on until she had reached the landing at the top of the stairs. The news she brought, of which she never ran short, was devoid of the slightest possible interest, especially when she held forth, as she was very prone to do, about personages in high and the highest places. Her favorite topic was the little prin-

cesses of the royal family: *la petite Princesse Charlotte
et la petite Princesse Alexandrine*,[2] whom she would
occasionally meet in the apartments of a French gov-
erness friend of hers and toward whom she felt such
close ties of loyalty that when one day the guard at
Brandenburg Gate, as *la Princesse Alexandrine* was driving past, had failed to present arms and to beat the
drum in time, she not only shared the universal sense of
outrage at the incident but, what was more, looked upon
it as though an earthquake had been visited on Berlin.

Such was the little aunt who had just come in.

Frau von Carayon went up to greet her affectionately,
with a greater show of affection it may be than was her
wont, for the simple reason that the aunt's arrival had
cut short a conversation that she herself had no longer
had sufficient strength of mind to terminate. Aunt Marguerite was quick to perceive by the tone how auspicious was the lie of the land for her today and as soon as
she had sat down and put her silk gloves into her reti-
cule turned to the subject of the highly placed personages at the royal estates, but this time omitting any
reference to those in "the highest places." Her accounts
of the life of the nobility were as a rule greatly to be
preferred to her anecdotes about life at court and would
invariably have passed muster but for her defect of
treating the after all crucial question of personalities
with an utmost disdain. That is to say, she would consistently get the names mixed up, and when she described some escapade of Baroness Stieglitz it was safe
to assume that it was Countess Taube she was thinking

of. Such news also opened the conversation today, of which the item "that Cavalry Captain von Schenk of the Garde du Corps Regiment had treated Princess von Croy to a serenade" was by far the most important one, especially when it turned out after some interrogatory to and fro that Captain von Schenk needed to be transformed into Captain von Schach, the Garde du Corps into the Gensdarmes Regiment, and Princess von Croy into Princess von Carolath. Such corrections would always be accepted by the aunt without a trace of embarrassment and she was equally immune to such embarrassment *today* when told after she had finished her story that Captain von Schenk *alias* Schach was expected in the course of the afternoon, as they had arranged for a drive into the country with him. Perfect gentleman that he was, he was sure to be delighted at the prospect of a cherished member of the family being included in this excursion. A remark that was received very graciously by Aunt Marguerite and attended by an involuntary tugging at her taffeta dress.

On the stroke of three they had sat down to dinner, and on the stroke of four—*l'exactitude est la politesse des rois,*[3] as Bülow would have said—a chaise with its top folded back drew up in front of the house in the Behrenstrasse. Schach, who was driving himself, was about to hand the reins to the groom, but both Carayons were already waving to him from the balcony, ready to start, and, equipped with a complete supply of kerchiefs, parasols, and umbrellas, presently appeared at the carriage door below. Aunt Marguerite was with them, too, whom they introduced and who was greeted by Schach with his peculiar blend of deference and grandeur.

"And now for the obscure destination, Fräulein Victoire."

"Let's settle on Tempelhof," she said.

"Well chosen. Only, forgive me, it's the least obscure destination on earth. Sun and more sun."

They drove down Friedrichstrasse at a brisk trot, at first in the direction of the round flower bed and Halle Gate until the soft, marshy road that led up to the Kreuzberg compelled them to a slower pace. Schach felt he ought to apologize, but Victoire, seated with her back to him and by half turning around freely able to talk to him, was genuinely thrilled as a true child of the city by everything she saw on both sides of the road. She did not cease plying him with questions, and by the curiosity she evinced dispelled his misgivings. What amused her more than anything was the stuffed figures of grotesquely dressed old women scattered about the bushes and garden beds either in poke bonnets of straw or with curl papers flapping and fluttering in the wind.

Finally they had reached the top of the slope and, following the hard mud road lined with poplar trees, they jogged on more quickly again in the direction of Tempelhof. Alongside the road, kites were rising up in the sky, swallows were darting to and fro, and the church spires of the nearest villages were glistening on the horizon.

Aunt Marguerite, blown about in the wind, was forever trying to keep the little collar of her overcoat in place. She insisted, nevertheless, on acting as guide and startled the two Carayon ladies by muddling up names and discovering resemblences that did not exist.

"Take a look at the steeple of that Wilmersdorf church, Victoire dear. Isn't it like our church in Dorotheenstadt?"

Victoire made no reply.

"I don't mean on account of its spire, Victoire dear, but on account of its main structure."

Both ladies were dismayed. But the upshot of it was what it usually is, that is, what is embarrassing to those immediately concerned is ignored or shrugged off by those indirectly affected. And now Schach of all people! He was too much of a seasoned habitué of the world of elderly princesses and ladies-in-waiting to be particularly astonished at any manifestation of stupidity or ignorance. He just smiled and seized on the reference to the "church in Dorotheenstadt" to ask Frau von Carayon "whether she had ever gone to see the monument that the late King of most blessed memory had had erected to his son, Count von der Mark,[4] in the church in question."

Mother and daughter replied in the negative. Aunt Marguerite, on the other hand, who never liked to admit *not* knowing something, let alone not having seen it, remarked in a general kind of way:

"Oh, the dear little Prince. That he had to die so young. What a wretched business. And took so after her ladyship his mother of most blessed memory in the expression about the eyes."

For a moment it seemed as though Schach, deeply affronted in his feelings about legitimacy, was about to comment and scornfully make short shrift of any dynastic claim of the "dear little Prince" born of that "mother of most blessed memory." However, he at once realized the foolishness of any such thought and, so as to be doing something at least, pointed out the green dome of Charlottenburg Castle looming up just then, and presently turned into the village street of Tempelhof bordered by old linden trees.

The next house but one was an inn. Handing the reins to the groom, he jumped down in order to help the ladies out of the carriage. But only Frau von Carayon gratefully accepted his offer, while Aunt Marguerite politely declined, "having learned that reliance on one's own hands always was best."

The fine weather had attracted the guests in large numbers outdoors so that all the tables in the fenced-in front garden were taken. Thus they found themselves in somewhat of a predicament. But just as they had decided to have their coffee in the back garden under the roof of a bowling-alley shed standing half open, one of the corner tables became vacant so that they were able to remain in the front garden with its view of the village street. They did so, and it happened to be the prettiest table. A maple rose up from its center and although, except at the outer tips here and there, it was not yet adorned by any foliage, birds were already perching on its branches and chirping. And *this* was not the only thing they saw. Carriages were stopping in the middle of the village street, the city coachmen were engrossed

in chats, and peasants and farmhands, fresh from the
field with harrow and plow, were making their way
along the row of carriages. Lastly, a flock of sheep appeared on the scene which the sheep dog, now from
their right, now from their left flank, kept in formation,
and intermittently the bell ringing for evensong was
making itself heard. For it was just six o'clock.

The Carayons, pampered city dwellers though they
were, or perhaps even *because* of it, reacted enthusiasti-
cally to everything and exclaimed with delight when
Schach suggested an evening stroll to the church at
Tempelhof. Sunset was the finest hour. Aunt Marguerite, afraid of the "silly cattle," would of course have
preferred to stay behind at her table, but when the inn-
keeper, summoned to add a calming word, had assured
her in the most emphatic terms "that she needn't be
afraid of the bull," she took Victoire's arm and went out
into the village street with her, while Schach and Frau
von Carayon brought up the rear. Those still sitting by
the picket fence followed them with their eyes.

" 'There's naught so finely spun . . . ,' "[5] Frau von
Carayon said, laughing.

Schach eyed her with a puzzled look.

"Yes, dear friend, I'm informed about everything. And
no less a person than Aunt Marguerite has told us about
it this noon."

"About what?"

"About the serenade. Madame Carolath is a woman of
the world and above all a princess. And you know, don't
you, what they say about you preferring the ugliest

princess to the most attractive bourgeoise. An ugly princess, I say. But Princess Carolath happens to be attractive into the bargain as well. *Un teint de lys et de rose.*[6] You're going to make me jealous."

Schach kissed the beautiful lady's hand.

"Aunt Marguerite has informed you correctly, and you're to hear everything, down to the smallest detail. For if I enjoy, as I confess I do, counting such an evening as part of my experience, I enjoy even more being able to talk about it to my beautiful friend. It's just because of the teasing way you have, so critical and so good-natured at the same time, that I come to appreciate and value everything. You needn't smile. Oh, if only I could tell you everything. Dear Josephine, you represent the paragon of a woman for me: intelligent and yet with nothing of the bluestocking and free of conceit, full of *élan* and yet not given to mockery. The affections of my *heart* are meant, as they have always been, only for you, you the kindest and worthiest of all. And the most charming thing about you, dear friend, is that you don't even realize how good you are and what a tacit influence you exert on me."

He had spoken almost with feeling, and the beautiful lady's eyes lit up, while her hand lay trembling in his. But she was quick to revert to her bantering tone, saying:

"How good you are at eloquence. Do you know, such eloquence can only be the prompting of some offense."

"Or of the heart. But let's leave it at some offense that calls for expiation. And first of all for confession. That's what I came for yesterday. I had forgotten it was your soirée and nearly had a shock seeing Bülow and that puffed-up plebeian Sander. How ever does he manage to find his way into your circle?"

"He's Bülow's shadow."

"An odd shadow that's three times the weight of the object it reflects. A regular mammoth. Only his wife's said to go him one better, which explains the sardonic remark I heard the other day: Sander when going for his walk to take the waters would merely walk three times in an orbit around his wife. And this man Bülow's shadow! If instead you'd said his Sancho Panza . . ."

"Then you regard Bülow himself as Don Quixote?"

"Yes, madam . . . You know how I ordinarily hate speaking disparagingly of anyone, but this isn't any disparagement when you come down to it, it's more like flattery. The brave Knight of La Mancha was an honest-to-goodness enthusiast, but can the same be said of Bülow? I ask you, dear friend. Enthusiast, indeed! He's an eccentric, nothing else, and the fire that burns in him is simply that of infernal self-love."

"You misjudge him, dear Schach. He's embittered, granted, but I'm afraid he has reason to be."

"Anyone afflicted with morbid conceit will always have a thousand and one reasons for feeling embittered. He migrates from one social set to another, preaching the most hackneyed of wisdoms, the wisdom of hindsight. Preposterous. All that we've had to put up with in the way of humiliations during the past year is due, if you listen to him, not to the arrogance or power of our enemies, oh, no, that power could have been opposed effectively enough by superior power if our, that's to say Bülow's, ingenuity had been mobilized in good time. That's what the world failed to do, and that's its undoing. And so on *ad infinitum*. Hence Ulm and hence Austerlitz.[7] Everything would have taken on a different complexion, turned out differently, if the Corsican usurper of throne and crown, this angel of darkness who calls himself Bonaparte, had found himself confronted on the battlefield by that creature of light, Bülow. I find this odious. I loathe such braggadocio. He speaks of Brunswick[8] and Hohenlohe[9] as though they were ludicrous figures, but *I* stand by the Frederickian axiom that the world rests no more securely on the shoulders of Atlas than does Prussia on those of her army."

While this conversation between Schach and Frau von Carayon was taking place, the pair walking ahead of them had come to a point in the road where a footpath branched off across a freshly plowed field.

"There's the church," said the aunt, pointing with her parasol to the newly tiled roof of a tower, its red color gleaming through all kinds of bushes and branches. Victoire acknowledged what was in any case not open to dispute, at the same time looking back to ask her mother by a motion of her head and hand whether they were to take the footpath that branched off at this point. Frau von Carayon gave an affirmative nod, and the aunt and Victoire proceeded in the direction indicated. From all over the brown field larks were taking to the air, having built their nests in the furrows even before the crop was out. Finally, they came to a barren stretch of land that extended right up to the churchyard wall and was marked, apart from a patch of grass, only by a little crater-shaped puddle in which a pair of toads were practicing their tunes, screened by a fringe of tall rushes.

"Look, Victoire, they're rushes."

"Yes, auntie, dear."

"Are *you* able to imagine, *ma chère*, that when I was young rushes were used as little bedside lights and, sure enough, they'd merrily float about in a glass when one was ill or just couldn't go to sleep . . ."

"I certainly can," replied Victoire, who never contradicted her aunt, and at the same time kept her ears cocked toward the puddle where the toads were striking up ever noisier tunes. But presently she saw a young girl running toward her at full speed from the direction of the church and romping with a shaggy-haired, white Pomeranian dog which, barking and snapping, kept jumping up at the child. As she ran, the girl threw a church-door key dangling from a rope and peg up in the air and caught it again so skillfully as to avoid being hurt by either the key or the peg. At last she stopped, shading her eyes with her left hand, blinded by the setting sun.

"Are you the sexton's daughter?" Victoire asked.

"Yes, I am," said the girl.

"Then, please let us have the key, or come with us and unlock the door for us again. We'd like to take a look at the church, we and the lady and gentleman over there."

"Certainly," said the girl and ran ahead of them, climbed over the churchyard wall and soon disappeared behind the hazel and hawthorn bushes which grew here in such profusion that, though still bare, they formed a dense hedge.

The aunt and Victoire followed her, picking their way over dilapidated graves which had so far been left wholly untouched by spring. There wasn't a leaf to be seen, only immediately alongside the church there was a shady-dank spot as of a carpet of violets. Bending down, Victoire quickly plucked some of them, and when presently Schach and Frau von Carayon came up the regular main churchyard path, Victoire went up to them and handed her mother the violets.

The girl had meanwhile unlocked the church and was sitting on the doorstep, waiting. When both couples approached, she got up and, leading the way, entered the church whose choir stalls were almost as askew as the gravestones outside. Everything produced an effect of shabbiness and decay. Yet the orb of the sun setting behind the windows facing the evening sky bathed the walls in a crimson glow and, momentarily at least, restored the gilt long since faded of the old, sacred altar figures which, relics of the Catholic era, were surviving there. Inevitably, the aunt, of Calvinist persuasion, was genuinely dismayed when she caught sight of these "idols." Schach, for his part, whose hobbies included genealogy, asked the girl whether there might not perhaps be some old tombstones about.

"There's one," she said. "This one," and indicated a

smooth-worn, though still clearly recognizable effigy in stone set in an upright position in a pillar close by the altar. It was unmistakably a cavalry commander.

"And who is it?" Schach asked.

"A Knight Templar,"[10] said the girl, "and called the Knight of Tempelhof. And he had his tombstone made even during his lifetime, because he wanted to become like it."

The aunt nodded approvingly at this point, because the need for an image to conform to on the part of the putative Knight of Tempelhof struck a sympathetic chord in her heart.

"And he built this church," the girl continued, "and finally built the village as well, calling it Tempelhof, because he was called Tempelhof himself. And the Berliners say 'Templov.' But that's wrong."

The ladies listened attentively to all this, and only Schach, whose curiosity had been aroused, went on to inquire "if she couldn't tell them about another incident or two in his life."

"No, not about his life. But about later on."

They all pricked up their ears, especially the aunt, who was immediately seized by a slight shiver. But the girl went on in a calm tone:

"Whether it all happened as people say it did I don't know. But old farmer Maltusch was there to see it all at the time."

"See what, child?"

"He'd been lying here in front of the altar for over a hundred years until he got tired of the peasants and the children who were going to be confirmed always tramping about on top of him and wearing his face smooth with their scraping feet on their way to communion. And old Maltusch, who's close to ninety now, told my father and me he'd heard it with his own ears—such rumbling and rolling it made you think it was thundering over in Schmargendorf."

"Quite possible."

"But they couldn't understand what that rumbling and rolling meant," the girl continued. "And so it went until the year that the Russian general,[11] whose name I always forget, was buried in the churchyard here in Tempelhof. Then one Saturday, the former sexton here wanted to erase the numbers of the hymns and write out new ones for Sunday. And had picked up the chalk. Then he suddenly saw that the numbers had already been erased and new ones been put up and also those of a Biblical passage with chapter and verse. And all of it in old-fashioned writing and blurred so that one could only just make it out. And when they looked it up they read: 'You shall honor the memory of your dead and not disfigure their face.' And now they realized who'd written out those numbers and they pulled up the slab and cemented it into this pillar."

"I honestly think," said Aunt Marguerite who, the greater her terror of ghosts the more she denied their existence, "I honestly think the Government ought to do more to combat superstition."

So saying, she nervously turned away from the mysterious statue and together with Frau von Carayon, who when it came to fear of ghosts could hold her own with the aunt, made for the exit.

Schach followed with Victoire whom he had offered his arm.

"Was it really a Knight Templar?" Victoire asked. "My knowledge of Knights Templars is of course limited to the *one* in Lessing's *Nathan the Wise*. But if our stage hasn't been too free in the matter of dress, the Knights Templars must have looked decidedly different. Am I right?"

"*Always* right, my dear Victoire."

And the tone of this remark touched her heart and evoked a quivering echo without Schach being aware of it.

"Well, then. But if not a Knight Templar, what *else*?" she pressed on, turning to him with a tender and yet puzzled look.

"A cavalry commander of the time of the Thirty Years' War. Or perhaps going back no further than the period of Fehrbellin.[12] I even read the name: Achim von Haake."

"Then you think the whole story is a fairy tale?"

"Not in so many words, or at least not altogether. It's an established fact that we did have Knights Templars in these parts. And this church with its pre-Gothic style may very well date back to the days of the Templars. So much one can accept."

"I so enjoy hearing about this order."

"So do I. It was the one made to suffer most at the hands of divine retribution and for that reason is the most poetic and interesting one. You know what it is taxed

with: idolatry, denial of Christ, vice of every description.
And rightly so, I'm afraid. But however great its offense,
its expiation was on the same scale, quite apart from the
fact that this too was a case of the innocent descendant
being made to atone for the sins of the past generations.
The fate and destiny of all institutions which, even where
they blunder and transgress, deviate from the ordinary
everyday path. And so we see the guilt-stained order,
irrespective of its whole record of disgrace, ultimately
come to grief within the restored halo of its fame. It was
envy that destroyed it, envy and selfishness, and whether
it was to blame or not, I stand in awe of its stature."

Victoire smiled.

"Anyone hearing you talk like this, dear Schach, would
think he could detect a latter-day Knight Templar in you.
And yet it was a monastic order and its vow, too, was a
monastic one. Would you've been able to live and die
like a Knight Templar?"

"Yes, I would."

"Perhaps tempted by their garb, which was even more
becoming than the tunic of the Gensdarmes."

"Not by their garb, Victoire. You misjudge me. Believe
me, there's some vital spark in me that won't let me shrink
from any vow."

"And hold to it?"

But before he had a chance to reply, she quickly continued in a more playful tone:

"I think Philip the Fair[13] has the order on his conscience. Curious that I have a dislike of all historical figures
nicknamed 'the *Fair*.' And not, I trust, out of envy. But

good looks—that must be so—make for selfishness, and to be selfish is to be devoid of loyalty and gratitude."

Schach tried to contradict her. He realized that Victoire's remarks, however fond she was of piquant hints and innuendoes, could not conceivably have been aimed at *him*. And there he was quite right. It was all just *jeu d'esprit*, an indulgence on her part of a propensity to philosophize. And yet everything she had said, for all that it had clearly been said without anything being meant by it, had no less clearly been uttered out of some dim presentiment.

By the time they had ceased arguing they had come to the edge of the village, and Schach stopped to wait for Frau von Carayon and Aunt Marguerite, who had both fallen behind.

When they had caught up, he offered Frau von Carayon his arm and escorted *her* back to the inn.

Victoire gazed after them, baffled, pondering the exchange which Schach had let pass without a word of apology. "What was going on?" And she changed color when, seized by a sudden suspicion, she had answered her own question.

There was no longer any thought of sitting down at a table in front of the inn, which they were all the more willing to forgo as it had meanwhile turned cool and the wind that had been blowing all day had veered round to a northwesterly direction.

Aunt Marguerite asked to be allowed to sit in the back seat "so as not to be traveling facing the wind."

Nobody objected. She therefore took the seat she had

requested and while everybody was silently absorbed in reflecting on the special significance of the afternoon for him or her, they drove back to the city at rapidly accelerating pace.

The city lay already wrapped in dusk when they reached the slope of the Kreuzberg and only the two domes of the Gensdarmes towers still rose up through the bluish-gray mist.

V

Victoire von Carayon to Lisette von Perbandt

Ma chère Lisette:

I was so delighted to hear from you at long last, and such
good news. Not that I would have expected it to be otherwise. I have met few men who so in every way seem to me to
be a guarantee of happiness as your husband. Level-headed,
kindly, modest, and with that nicely balanced proportion of
knowledge and breeding which steers clear of any equally
hazardous too much and too little, of which the "too much"
may conceivably be the yet more hazardous. For young
women are only too prone to insist: "You shall have no other
gods besides me." I see this almost daily among the Rombergs,
and Marie is not particularly grateful to her clever and genial
husband for neglecting in his concern with politics and
French newspapers their social rounds and his toilette.

The only thing that caused me some worry was your new Masurian homeland, a region I always used to imagine as one huge forest with a hundred lakes and swamps. I was therefore afraid that this new homeland might throw you into a state of melancholy daydreaming, which in such situations is always the prelude to homesickness or even to depression and tears. And that, so I'm told, men find upsetting. But I'm ever so happy to hear that you have escaped *this* danger as well and that the birches enclosing your château are greening rather than weeping birches. By the way, you must write to me about the birch wine some time. It's one of those things I have always been curious about, but which I have never had the good fortune to come across up to now.

And now I must tell you about *us*. You thoughtfully inquire about all and sundry and even ask to hear about Aunt Marguerite's latest princess and muddling up of names. I could tell you especially about *that*, since it's less than three days that we had (at least as far as these muddles are concerned) more than our fair share of it.

The occasion was a drive into the country on which we were taken by Herr von Schach, to Tempelhof, and for which Aunt Marguerite had to be asked as well, as it happened to be her day. You know that on Tuesdays we always have her with us as our guest. She therefore also came to the church with us where at the sight of some pictures of saints dating from the Catholic era she not only kept hammering away at the need to get rid of superstition root and branch, but persisted in addressing herself with this very demand also to Schach as though he were a member of the consistory. And now as I write (given as I am to the virtue or vice of always immediately visualizing everything large as life) I put down my pen, shaking with laughter. Actually, though, it's not nearly so absurd as it seems at first glance. He does have an air of consistorial solemnity about him, and if I'm not completely mistaken, it's precisely this air of solemnity that turns Bülow so sharply against him. Infinitely more so than their divergence of views.

And it almost sounds as though in describing it like this I were joining forces with Bülow. Indeed, if you weren't so well acquainted with the facts, you'd never guess from this picture of him what a high regard I have for him. More so than ever really, even though there's no lack of many a painful aspect. But in my position one learns to be charitable, resigned, forgiving. If I had *not* learned it, how would I be able to live, *I*, who am so fond of life! An indulgence (as I once read) said to be common among those in whom one can least account for it.

But I have spoken of many a painful aspect and am longing to tell you about it.

It arose only yesterday on our outing. As we made our way from the village to the church, Schach escorted Mama. Not by accident, it had been so arranged, that is, by *me*. I let them fall behind, because I wanted to give them an opportunity for a heart-to-heart talk (you know what *kind*). Peaceful evenings like that when one wanders across the fields and the only sounds one hears are the peals of the evensong bell lift us above the trivial constraints of convention and make us feel more at ease. And once in *that* state, we are sure to strike the right note. What was discussed between them I don't know, certainly not *that* which should have been discussed. Finally, we went inside the church which was as though bathed in the sunset glow, everything was throbbing with life, and it was of an unforgettable beauty.

On the way home, Schach changed over and escorted *me*. He spoke in a very captivating way and in a tone as gratifying as it was unexpected. Every word of it is engraved in my memory and provides food for thought. But what happened? When we got back to the edge of the village, he became increasingly reticent and waited for Mama. Then he offered his arm to *her*, and so they walked back through the village to the inn where the carriages were drawn up and a large number of people were gathered. I felt a stab in my heart, for I could not help thinking that he would have found it embarrassing to appear with *me* and on my arm among the guests. With all his vanity, of which I can't acquit him, it is beyond him to shrug off people's gossip, and a sardonic smile puts him out of humor for a week. Self-possessed as he is, in that *one* respect he is no less weak and susceptible. There isn't a soul in the world, not even Mama, to whom I could so freely admit this, but to *you* I must. If I'm being unfair, tell me that my misfortune has made me distrustful, lecture me without the slightest mincing of words and you may be sure that I shall read them with an appreciative eye. For in spite of all his vanity, I value him as I don't anyone else. There's a dictum that men mustn't be vain, because vanity is supposed to invite ridicule. This strikes me as an exaggeration. But if the dictum is valid all the same, then Schach represents an exception. I hate the word "chivalrous" and yet can't think of any other for him. One quality may be even more marked in him, discretion, a presence that commands respect, or at any rate a natural air of distinction, and if what I want for both Mama's and my own sake should come true, I could without difficulty arrive at an attitude of filial devotion toward him.

And one more point. You never thought of him as very intelligent, and I for my part merely used to counter with timid dissent. Even so, his is the best kind of intelligence, the intermediate range, what's more, the one that goes with the man of integrity. This is always brought home to me in his feuds with Bülow. Much as the latter may surpass him, he nevertheless comes off second best. Moreover, I'm surprised sometimes how the anger bubbling up in our friend lends him a certain gift for quick repartee, even downright wit. Yesterday he referred to Sander, whose personality you know, as Bülow's Sancho Panza. All that's implied by this is obvious, and I think it's not bad.

Sander's publications are creating more of a stir than ever; times are conducive to purely polemical writings. Besides Bülow's there have been papers by Massenbach and Phull,[1] which are being extolled by the experts as something extraordinary and unprecedented. It's all directed against Austria and proves once again that insult is the twin of injury. Schach is indignant at this overweening conceit, as he calls it, and has taken up his old hobbies again, engravings and race horses. His diminutive groom is becoming more and more diminutive. What in Chinese women is represented by their tiny feet has its counterpart in grooms in their miniature proportions as such. Personally, I disapprove of both, especially of the tiny feet tight-laced in Chinese fashion and, on the contrary, am happy in my comfortable slippers. I would never use them to rule the roost with them, something I'm content to leave to my dear Lisette. Do it with your characteristic gentle touch. Remember me to your husband, whose only fault is that he took you away from me. Mama sends love and kisses to her pet, but I leave you with the earnest wish that with the rich harvest of happiness you have reaped you won't *completely* forget the one who, as you know, hopes for no more than a rightful share of that happiness.

Your Victoire

VI

At Prince Louis's

On the same evening on which Victoire von Carayon wrote her letter to Lisette von Perbandt, Schach received an invitation in Prince Louis's hand at his lodgings in the Wilhelmstrasse.

It read:

Dear Schach:

I have been here in the countryside of Moabit[1] for only three days and am already starving for some company and conversation. To be a quarter of a mile from the capital is quite enough to make one feel out of touch with it and hanker after it. May I count on your coming tomorrow? Bülow and his publishing appendage have accepted, so have Massenbach and Phull. In other words, no one but the Opposition, who cheer me up, even though I cross swords with them. From your regiment, you will be meeting Nostitz and Alvensleben. Casual dress uniform and at five o'clock.

Yours,

Louis, Prince of Prussia

At the appointed hour, Schach, having collected Alvensleben and Nostitz, drove up to the Prince's villa. It was situated on the right bank of the river, surrounded by meadows and willows, and, overlooking the Spree, faced the western edge of the Zoological Gardens. Driveway and stairs provided access from the rear. A wide, carpeted staircase led to a landing and from there to a lobby where the guests were received by the Prince. Bülow and Sander had already arrived, whereas Massenbach and Phull had asked to be excused. It suited Schach; he found even Bülow more than enough and had no desire to see the ranks of the luminaries augmented. It was still broad daylight, yet the lights in the dining hall which they entered from the vestibule were already lit and the shutters (as it happened, with the windows open) were closed. A harmonious complement to this display of artificial light, intermingled with an intruding glint of daylight from outside, was the fire on the hearth in the center of the hall. The Prince, his back to them, was sitting directly in front of it, peering through the small open slats at the trees in the Zoological Gardens.

"I must ask you to put up with things," he opened the conversation when the guests had sat down at table. "We're out in the country here, so that you must excuse all the shortcomings. *A la guerre comme à la guerre.*[2] Massenbach, by the way, our gourmet, must have suspected, or perhaps feared, something like this. Which certainly wouldn't surprise me. It's not for nothing, dear Sander, that your commendable table even more than your commendable publishing house is credited with cementing the friendship between you."

"A statement I would scarcely venture to deny, Royal Highness."

"And yet you really *ought to*. Your whole publishing enterprise is without a trace of that laissez faire which is the prerogative, indeed the duty, of all well-fed souls. All your geniuses (beg your pardon, Bülow) write as though they were starving. As you please. Our parade-ground gents you may keep, but that you're treating the Austrians so shabbily, too, I resent."

"Am *I* to blame, Royal Highness? I, for my part, don't pretend to know anything about grand strategy. At the same time, of course, in my capacity as a publisher, as it were, I'd like to raise the question, 'Was Ulm an intelligent move?' "

"Ah, my dear Sander, what's intelligent? We Prussians always fancy we are. And d'you know what Napoleon said about the way we'd drawn up our formations in Thuringia last year? You repeat it for him, Nostitz . . . He won't. Well, then I have to do it myself. 'Ah, *ces Prussiens*,' it went, '*ils sont encore* plus *stupides que les Autrichiens*.'[3] There's an opinion of our vaunted intelligence for you, what's more, an opinion from the most highly qualified quarters. And if he did hit it exactly here, we'd do well after all to congratulate ourselves on the peace terms Haugwitz sold out for on our behalf. Yes, sold out, sacrificing our honor for a trinket. Of what use is Hanover to us? It's the crumb on which the Prussian eagle is going to choke."

"I rate the swallowing and digestive capacity of our Prussian eagle higher," Bülow retorted. "That's just what he's specially good at and has been an old hand at from time immemorial. Still, on *this* point there's room for argument, but what does *not* admit of any argument is the peace agreement Haugwitz has procured for us. It's as vital to us as our daily bread, much as we value our life. Royal Highness has of course an aversion to poor Haugwitz, which surprises me, inasmuch as Lombard,[4] who is after all the moving spirit behind the whole business, has always been regarded with favor by Your Royal Highness."

"Ah, Lombard! I don't take Lombard seriously and, besides, tax him with being half-French. Then, too, he's got what, with me, proves a disarming sense of humor. You know, don't you, his father was a hairdresser and his wife's father, a barber. And now that wife of his, who's not only vain enough to drive you up the wall but also writes execrable French verse, comes along and wants to know which was the more telling phrase: '*L'hirondelle* frise *la surface des eaux*' or '*L'hirondelle* rase *la surface des eaux?*'[5] And what does he reply? 'I can see no difference, my dear. *L'hirondelle* frise is a tribute to *my* father and *l'hirondelle* rase, to *yours*.' This witticism sums up Lombard in a nutshell for you. Speaking personally, I freely admit I can't resist such tongue-in-cheek self-mockery. He's a rogue, not a man of quality."

"Perhaps the same might be said about Haugwitz both in a laudatory and in a derogatory sense. And frankly, I'd be glad to let Your Royal Highness dispose of the *Man*, though *not* of his policy. His policy is sound, for it takes realistic account of things as they are. And Your Royal Highness is better informed about this than I am. And what assets can we draw on when all is said and done? We live from hand to mouth, and why? Because the state of Frederick the Great is not a country with an army but an army with a country. Our country is no more than a military base and supply center. In and by itself it is without any resources to speak of. As long as we win, things go tolerably well, but waging war is only open to countries that can afford to suffer defeat. We *can't*. Once the army's finished, everything's finished. And how quickly an army can be finished was shown us by Austerlitz. A puff of air is enough to destroy us, especially *us*. 'He blew with His wind, and the armada was scattered to the four winds.' *Afflavit Deus et dissipati sunt*."

"Herr von Bülow," Schach broke in at this point, "will give me leave for a comment. He doesn't, I trust, propose to equate the hellish fumes currently sweeping across the world with the breath of God, not with *that* which blew the armada to bits."

"I do indeed, Herr von Schach. Or do you seriously believe that the breath of God is at the special beck and call of Protestantism or even of Prussia and her army?"

"I hope it is."

"And I'm afraid it's *not*. We've got the 'neatest army,' that's as far as it goes. But you're not going to win battles with 'neatness.' Does Your Royal Highness remember the remark by the Great King when General Lehwald[6] had his regiments, three times defeated, pass before him in review? 'A neat lot,' he said. 'Take a look at mine. They look like tramps, but they bite.' I fear we've got too many Lehwald regiments these days and too few of the Old Man's. The spirit's gone, everything has degenerated into drill and make-believe. Think of those officers who, just to flaunt the sinews of bulging muscle and limb, have taken to wearing their uniform next to their skin. It's all affectation. Even marching, that ordinary everyday human command of one's legs, has in the course of the perpetual goose-stepping become for us a lost art. And the art of marching is nowadays a prerequisite for success. All modern battles have been won with the legs."

"And with *gold*," the Prince interrupted. "Your great *Empereur*, dear Bülow, is especially partial to the use of small change, yes, even of the smallest amounts. That he's a liar goes without saying. But he's also a past master at bribery. And who opened our eyes to it? He himself. Read what he said immediately before the battle of Austerlitz. 'Soldiers,' he announced, 'the enemy is going to march and try to smash our flank, but he'll be paying for this flanking movement with a smashed flank of his own. We'll hurl ourselves at that exposed flank of his, and beat and crush him.' And that was exactly how the battle went. It's inconceivable that he could have deduced the Austrians' plan of campaign simply from the way they had drawn up their troops."

They all fell silent. But since the effusive Prince found

this silence a good deal more embarrassing than any contradiction, he turned directly to Bülow, saying:

"Refute what I've just said."

"Royal Highness commands, and so I'll obey. The Emperor foresaw precisely what was going to happen, was *able* to foresee it, because by calculating in advance 'how would *mediocrity* proceed in a situation like this?,' he had not only posed but also answered the question. Supreme stupidity, admittedly, defies calculation as much as does supreme intelligence—this is one of the cardinal criteria of genuine and unadulterated stupidity. But the 'middling bright,' who are just bright enough to want to try their hand at something intellectually challenging for once, these middling bright are always the most predictable. And why? Because they invariably confine themselves to swimming with the tide and ape today the ways observed yesterday. And the Emperor was aware of all this. *Hic haeret.*[7] He never acquitted himself more brilliantly than he did in that operation at Austerlitz, not even excepting minor engagements, nor yet those impromptus and flashes of humor in the realm of terror that after all reveal the true stamp of genius."

"An example."

"One must stand for a hundred. When the central sector of the front was already breached, part of the Russian Guard Regiment, four battalions, had retreated to as many frozen ponds, and a French battery was brought up to fire a volley of case shots into the battalions. At that very moment, the Emperor appeared. He grasped the special nature of the situation at a glance.

'Why bother with a piecemeal effort?' And he gave orders that a charge of solid iron balls be fired into the *ice*. A minute later, the ice burst and broke up, and all four battalions were sucked in battle array into the swampy depths. Such flashes of insight are only given to genius. The Russians will now decide that next time they'll do the same, but while Kutuzov[8] is waiting for ice, he'll suddenly find himself plunged into water or fire. All due credit to Austro-Russian bravery, only let's leave out their ingenuity. There's a passage[9] somewhere that goes: 'In my wolfskin pack the devil's sexton rears his head, a goblin, a genius'—well, no Russo-Austrian soldier's pack has ever yet harbored a goblin and devil's sexton. And to compensate for this deficiency, they fall back on the wretched, old face-saving explanations: bribery and treachery. The loser always finds it hard to seek the cause of his defeat in the appropriate location, that is, in *himself*, and Czar Alexander, too, I think, shrinks from such an investigation in the clearly most logical place."

"And who would blame him for it?" retorted Schach. "He did his duty, in fact, more than that. When the hill was already taken and on the other hand the possibility of retrieving the battle was not yet lost, he advanced, drums beating, at the head of fresh regiments. His horse was shot down from under him, he mounted another, and the battle raged in seesaw for half an hour. Veritable feats of bravery were performed, and the French themselves paid tribute to it in enthusiastic terms."

The Prince, who on the occasion of the Czar's visit[10]

to Berlin the year before, where he was invariably ac-
claimed as *deliciae generis humani*,[11] had not been too
favorably impressed with him, found it rather tiresome
to have the "kindest specimen of mankind" elevated to
the rank of "super hero" as well. It made him smile and
he said:

"With all due respect to His Imperial Majesty, I can't
help feeling, dear Schach, that you may be attaching
greater importance to French newspaper reports than
they deserve. The French are clever people. The more
they dramatize their enemy's fame, the more they stand
to enhance their own, and I'm passing over all sorts of
political motives which are surely a factor here. 'One
should make a bridge of gold for one's enemy,' as the
saying goes, and rightly so, since today's enemy may be
tomorrow's ally. Actually, some such machinations are
already in the air, indeed, if I'm correctly informed,
negotiations about a new division of the world are already in progress, I mean about a restoration of an East-
ern and Western Empire. But let's not worry our heads
about issues that are still pending and instead look for
an explanation of the eulogies of the Hero-Emperor
simply in the arithmetical proposition: 'If the bravery of
the Russians in defeat weighed a solid hundredweight,
then that of the French in victory weighed of course
two.' "

Schach, who had been wearing the Cross of St. Andrew[12] since Czar Alexander's visit to Berlin, was biting
his lips and about to reply, but Bülow forestalled him,
declaring:

"I'm anyhow always suspicious of 'imperial mounts shot down from under their riders.' And in this of all cases. The whole chorus of praise must have caused His Majesty acute embarrassment, since there are too many of those who can testify to the reverse. He's the 'good Czar' and that's enough."

"You say this in such a sarcastic tone, Herr von Bülow," replied Schach. "And yet I ask you, is there a finer epithet?"

"Oh, there certainly is. A *truly* great man is not lauded to the skies for his goodness, much less so referred to by name. On the contrary, he's apt to be a constant object of slander. For the rank and file, who universally predominate, only care for those on a par with them. Brenkenhof,[13] who for all his inconsistencies ought to be more widely read than he is, goes so far as to maintain that 'in our day and age the worthiest people are bound to enjoy the worst reputation.' The good Czar! Come now. Imagine how Frederick the Great would have rolled up his eyes if he'd been called the 'good Frederick.' "

"Bravo, Bülow," said the Prince, raising his glass in salute. "You've perfectly summed up my feelings."

But Bülow was in no need of this encouragement.

"All kings nicknamed the 'good,' " he pursued with mounting ardor, "are the kind that have led the kingdom entrusted to them to its doom or at any rate to the verge of revolution. The last king of Poland[14] was also a so-called 'good' one. Such royal personages are usually equipped with large harems and small brains. And when they're off to war, some Cleopatra must always tag along, whether with or without an asp."

"Surely, Herr von Bülow," Schach countered, "you don't suppose that by such statements as *these* you've described the essence of Czar Alexander?"

"At least roughly."

"Then I'd be curious to hear more."

"For that one only has to recall the Czar's last visit to Berlin and Potsdam. What was it all about? Well, admittedly about no trivial everyday sort of thing, but about the conclusion of an alliance that was a matter of life and death, and in point of fact they went by torchlight down into the vault of Frederick the Great to pledge themselves to a quasi-mystical blood brotherhood over his tomb. And what happened immediately afterward? Before three days had passed, it became known that the Czar, now happily emerged into daylight again from the vault of Frederick the Great, had divided the five most renowned beauties at court into as many categories of beauty: *beauté coquette*[15] and *beauté triviale*, *beauté céleste* and *beauté du diable*, and, finally, the fifth, '*beauté qui inspire seul du vrai sentiment*.' Which must have made everybody die of curiosity for a taste of that most exalted *vrai sentiment*."

VII

A New Arrival

All these sallies of Bülow's had aroused the mirth of
the Prince. In the impulsive way to which he was prone
he was about to launch into a disquisition on *beauté
céleste* and *beauté du diable* when he saw under the
portière, which was partly folded back, the short and
familiar figure of a gentleman with the unmistakable
demeanor of an artist emerge from the direction of the
corridor and presently enter the room.

"Ah, Dussek,[1] there's a good fellow," the Prince welcomed him. *Mieux vaut tard que jamais.*[2] Join us. Here.
And now let's put whatever's left of the sweets by our
artist friend. You'll find it's all still intact, dear Dussek.
No arguments. But what are you going to drink? You
name it. Asti, Montefiascone, Tokay."

"Some Hungarian wine."

"Dry?"

Dussek smiled.

"Silly question," the Prince corrected himself and in mounting good humor went on: "Well, now, Dussek, report. Theater people have, except for virtue itself, all kinds of virtues, including that of readiness of speech. They're rarely at a loss for an answer to the question, 'what's new?' "

"Nor are they today, Royal Highness," Dussek replied, stroking his tufted chin after taking a sip.

"Well, then, let's hear. What's the latest?"

"The whole town is in an uproar. By 'the whole town,' needless to say, I mean the theater."

"The theater *is* the town. So you're justified. And now go on."

"As Your Royal Highness commands. Well, then, we've been grossly insulted in the person of our leader and chief, and this has duly served to touch off what amounts to a little mutiny in the theater world. *That* then, it was said, was supposed to be the new era, *that* the bourgeois government, *that* the respect shown for Prussian 'belles lettres *et beaux arts.*' An 'homage to the arts'[3] was welcome, but an act of homage *hostile* to the arts was as unacceptable as ever."

"Dear Dussek," the Prince intervened, "with all due deference to your reflections, but inasmuch as you've invoked art, I must ask you not to overdo the art of suspense. More matter with less art, if you can. What's the point at issue?"

"Iffland is done for. He will *not* now be receiving the decoration in question."

Everybody laughed, most heartily of all Sander, and Nostitz declaimed:

"*Parturiunt montes, nascetur ridiculus mus.*"[4]

But Dussek was genuinely aroused and the hilarity of his audience only made it worse. He was particularly annoyed with Sander.

"You're laughing, Sander, although the only ones affected among present company are you and I. For at whom is the lance pointed if not at the bourgeoisie as such."

The Prince held out his hand to the speaker across the table.

"Well spoken, dear Dussek. I like such show of solidarity. Let's hear. How did it happen?"

"Above all, quite unexpectedly. Like a bolt from the blue. Royal Highness is aware that there had been talk of a citation for a long time, and putting aside any thought of fellow artists' envy, we'd been looking forward to it as though all of us were jointly going to receive and wear the decoration. Things, in fact, looked promising, and the production of *The Consecration of Strength*, in which the Court had expressed interest, was to provide both the impetus and special occasion. Iffland is a Freemason (*that*, too, gave us hope), the lodge actively promoted it, and the Queen's approval had been secured. And now it has fallen through *nevertheless*. A trifling matter, you'll say; but no, gentlemen, it's an important matter. Such things are always the straw that shows us which way the wind is blowing. And with us it keeps blowing, as usual, from the old direction. *Chi va piano, va sano*,[5] says the proverb. But in Prussia the motto is '*pianissimo.*' "

"Fallen through, you say, Dussek. But fallen through on account of what?"

"On account of the influence of the generals at Court. I've heard Rüchel's[6] name mentioned. Casting himself in the role of scholar, he pointed out in what a low regard the art of acting has been held by the world throughout history, with the sole exception of Nero's time. And *it* certainly couldn't serve as a model. That hit home. For what truly Christian king would care to be Nero or even hear the mention of his name. And so we are told that the matter has been shelved for the present. The Queen feels chagrined, and with this Sovereign chagrin we'll have to put up for the time being. New times and old prejudices."

"Dear *Kapellmeister*," said Bülow, "I'm sorry to see that your reflections are far ahead of your feelings. Which is the usual pattern, by the way. You speak of prejudices in which we're caught and are caught in them yourself. *You* and your whole bourgeoisie, which proposes to create not a new liberal social structure, but, envious and smug, merely to carve out a niche for itself among the old classes of privilege. But that won't get you anywhere. The petty jealousy that is gnawing away at the vitals of our third estate must be replaced by imperviousness to all these puerilities which have simply become obsolete. He who really forgets about ghosts, for him they've ceased to exist, and he who forgets about decorations works for their abolition. And so abolition of a veritable epidemic . . ."

"Just as Herr von Bülow, by contrast, is working for

the introduction of the utopias of the new kingdom," Sander broke in. "I for my part hold to the view that the malaise to which he refers will steadily continue to spread from east to west but not, conversely, abate in the direction from west to east. Rather, I have visions of ever new proliferations and a blossoming forth of a flora of decorations with twenty-four classes like the Linnaean system."

They all sided with Sander, most unequivocally so the Prince. There clearly was something in man's makeup which, such as fondness for jewelry and finery, also felt attracted by *this* ironmongery.

"Yes," he went on, "there's hardly a level of intelligence that's proof against it. You all no doubt look upon Kalckreuth[7] as an intelligent man, indeed, more than that, as a man who like few people must be imbued with the 'All is vanity' of our strivings and aims. And yet when he was awarded the Red Eagle, whereas he had been hoping for the Black one, he flung it, full of fury, into the drawer, shouting: 'Stay there until you're *black*.' A transformation of color that has since in fact come to pass."

"There's something odd about Kalckreuth," Bülow replied, "and, frankly, another of our generals who is supposed to have said, 'I'd offer the Black one if I could get rid of the Red one,' I like even better. Incidentally, I'm less finical than I may seem. There are also decorations which *not* to recognize as such would be downright small-minded or mean. Admiral Sir Sidney Smith, renowned for his defense of St. Jean d'Acre and disdainful of all decorations, did value one medal that the Bishop of Acre had presented to him with the words: 'We received this medal from the hands of Richard the Lion-hearted and after six hundred years are returning it to one of his compatriots who, with equal valor, secured the defense of our city.' And a cad and a fool he, I add, who would *not* find it in his heart to rejoice at *that* kind of decoration."

"I'm delighted to hear such remarks from your lips," the Prince replied. "It confirms me in my feelings for you, dear Bülow, and proves to me once again that— forgive me—the devil isn't nearly so black as he's painted."

The Prince was going to continue, but as one of the servants came up to him to inform him in a whisper that the table in the smoking room had been prepared and the coffee served, he rose from the table and led his guests, taking Bülow's arm, to the balcony outside the dining hall. A large, striped blue-and-white awning, its rings merrily rattling in the wind, had already been lowered. Beyond its dangling low fringe one had a view, upriver, of the city's spires partly shrouded in mist and, down-river, of the trees in the park of Charlottenburg with the sun setting behind the branches which were just turning green. They all stood in silent contemplation of the charming scene, and only when dusk had set in and a tall oil lamp been brought did they sit down and light their Dutch pipes, which each had chosen according to his particular taste. Only Dussek, mindful of the Prince's penchant for music, had stayed behind improvising on the grand piano in the dining hall, and all he saw when turning his head sideways were his table companions outside, once again engaged in more animated conversation, and the sparks thrown off by their clay pipes.

The conversation had reverted not to the subject of medals but to what had prompted it in the first place, that is, to Iffland and the impending production of the play. This led Alvensleben to say that he had become acquainted with some of the songs interpolated in the text during these last few days. Together with Schach. In fact, in the drawing room of Frau von Carayon and her daughter Victoire. The daughter had sung them and Schach had accompanied her.

"The Carayons," observed the Prince. "There isn't a name I keep hearing more often than *that* one. I had been told earlier about the two ladies by my good friend Pauline[8] and recently also by Rahel. It all conspires to arouse my curiosity and to make me seek for some clue, which I daresay won't be too hard to find. Don't I remember that charming young lady at Massov's children's ball[9] which, in the nature of all children's balls, enjoyed the distinction of serving as an altogether remarkable demonstration of adult and full-blown beauties. And when I say 'full-blown' I'm guilty of understatement. As a matter of fact, I've nowhere and at no time seen such striking beauties as at children's balls. It is as if rubbing shoulders with the consciously or unconsciously revolutionary-minded young acted as a twofold or threefold spur to those who for the moment are still at the helm to make their predominance felt, a predominance that by tomorrow may be a thing of the past. But anyhow, gentlemen, one may go so far as to say conclusively that children's balls only exist for the sake of adults, and tracing the causes of this intriguing phenomenon would really make a most suitable project for our Gentz.[10] Your philosophical friend Buchholz,[11] dear Sander, isn't subtle enough for my taste for such a game. You won't mind my saying so, by the way. He's your friend."

"But not to such an extent," Sander laughed, "that I wouldn't at any time gladly turn him over to Your Royal Highness. And as I may be permitted to add in this connection, not only for a most particular but also for an altogether general reason. For just as, in Your Royal Highness's opinion and experience, children's balls are really at their best without children, so friendships are best without friends. Substitutes are in any case absolutely everything in life and truly the ultimate quintessence of wisdom."

"Things must be in a very fair way with you, dear Sander," retorted the Prince, "that you can freely admit to such grotesque views. *Mais revenons à notre belle* Victoire.[12] She was one of the young ladies who led off the ceremony at the time with a series of tableaux vivants and, if my memory doesn't play me false, was cast in the role of Hebe as cupbearer to Zeus. Yes, that's how it was, and even as I'm talking about it, I can clearly see it again in my mind. She was barely fifteen, with the kind of waist that always seems to be on the point of breaking in two. But they never break. '*Comme un ange*,'[13] said old Count Neale, who was standing

next to me and boring me with an enthusiasm that
seemed to me just a caricature of my own. I should be
delighted if I might renew my acquaintance with the
ladies."

"Your Royal Highness wouldn't recognize Fräulein
Victoire," said Schach, none too pleased with the tone of
the Prince's remarks. "Immediately after the ball, she
came down with an attack of smallpox and only survived as if by a miracle. In her general appearance, to be
sure, she has retained a certain charm, but it's only at
odd moments that her singular sweetness of temper en-
velops her in a veil of beauty and seems to restore the
magic of her former days."

"Well, *restitutio in integrum*,"[14] said Sander.

They all laughed.

"If you want to put it like that, yes," replied Schach in
a caustic tone, ironically bowing to Sander.

The Prince discerned the note of ill humor and
wanted to dispel it.

"It's no use, dear Schach. You talk as though you
wanted to frighten me off, but your shot's gone badly
astray. Look here, what's beauty? One of the vaguest of
concepts. Must I remind you of the five categories that
we owe, first of all, to His Majesty Czar Alexander and,
secondly, to our friend Bülow? *Everything* is beautiful
and, then again, *nothing* is. Personally, I'd always give
first place to the *beauté du diable*, that's to say, to the
genre roughly corresponding to that of the once-beauti-
ful Fräulein von Carayon."

"Your Royal Highness will forgive me," Nostitz returned, "but I can't help feeling doubtful whether Your

Royal Highness would find any of the characteristics of the *beauté du diable* in Fräulein von Carayon. The young lady is given to a witty-elegiac tone, which at first glance seems to be a contradiction in terms and yet isn't, but which in any event may be thought to reflect her most distinctive trait. Don't you think so too, Alvensleben?"

Alvensleben agreed.

The Prince, on the other hand, inordinately fond as he was of doggedly pursuing the ins and outs of every question, gratified this tendency also today and continued with growing animation:

" 'Elegiac,' you say, 'witty-elegiac'; I couldn't imagine anything more aptly descriptive of a *beauté du diable*. You obviously interpret this concept in too narrow a sense, gentlemen. Everything associated with it in your mind is no more than a variation on the most common run-of-the-mill type of beauty, the *beauté coquette*: the dainty nose a little more turned up, the complexion a little darker in tone, the temperament a little more alert, the manners a little more oncoming and rash. But with this inventory you've by no means exhausted the higher form of the *beauté du diable*. It has about it a universal quality that far transcends the mere question of complexion and race. Just like the Catholic church. They're both oriented towards the inner life; and the inner life, on which in *our* argument everything turns, is called vigor, ardor, passion."

Nostitz and Sander nodded and smiled.

"Yes, gentlemen, I go further and repeat: 'What is

beauty?' Beauty, bah! Not only can the standard categories of beauty be dispensed with, their absence can
even be an outright advantage. In fact, dear Schach, I've
seen some astounding defeats and some even more
astounding victories. What happened at Morgarten and
Sempach[15] also applies in love, the handsome knights
are routed and the ugly peasants carry the day. Believe
me, the heart is what counts, *only* the heart. Who loves,
who possesses the power of love, is himself deserving of
love, and it would be grim if it were otherwise. Go
through the number of cases in your own experience.
What's a more common sight than that of an attractive
wife being supplanted by an unattractive mistress! And
this not at all according to the dictum *toujours perdrix.*[16]
Oh, no, the concatenations go much deeper than that.
The dullest thing in the world is the lymphatic-
phlegmatic *beauté*, the *beauté* par excellence. It's beset
by ailments now here, now there, I won't say always and
inevitably, but nevertheless in the majority of cases,
while my *beauté du diable* presents the very picture of
health, the kind of health on which in the last resort
everything depends and which is the equal of unsur-
passed charm. And now I ask you, gentlemen, who
stands to gain more by it than *that* constitution which
has passed, as though through purgatory, through the
most far-reaching and violent redemptive convulsions?
A cheek graced by a dimple or two is the most charming
thing there is, and this was thought to be so even in the
days of the Romans and Greeks, and I'm not so lacking
in gallantry and logic as to deny a multiplicity of dim-

ples the respect and tribute to which the single specimen or a little pair has from time immemorial been entitled. The paradox '*le laid c'est le beau*'[17] is completely
justified, and it means nothing else than that behind the
seemingly ugly there lurks a more rarefied form of
beauty. If my dear Pauline were here, as she unfortunately is *not*, she'd agree with me, freely and emphati-
cally, without being biased by any personal destinies."

The Prince fell silent. It was obvious that he was waiting for a collective expression of regret that Frau Pauline, who would sometimes act as hostess, was not
present today. But when nobody broke the silence, he
resumed:

"What we lack is women, and so the wine and our life
lack zest. I come back to my earlier request and repeat
that I'd be delighted at an opportunity to receive the
Carayon ladies in the drawing room of my friend. I
count on the gentlemen who belong to Frau von Carayon's circle to make themselves the spokesmen of my
request. You, Schach, or you, dear Alvensleben."

They both bowed.

"All things considered, it'll be best if my friend Pauline takes matters in hand herself. I suppose she'll be
calling on the Carayon ladies first, and I look forward to
hours of a most stimulating intellectual exchange."

The awkward silence with which these concluding
remarks, too, were received would have made itself felt
even more pointedly if Dussek had not come out to the
balcony just then.

"How beautiful," he burst out, his hand indicating the

horizon in the flaming yellow light that extended high up in to the western sky. The tall poplar trees stood out black and mute against the ribbon of yellow light, and even the dome of the palace was reduced to a silhouette.

Each of the guests was moved by the beauty of the scene. But the most beautiful sight was the numerous swans which, as everybody was looking up to the evening sky, were approaching in a long single file from the direction of Charlottenburg Park. Other swans had already taken up a forward position. It was obvious that the entire flotilla must have been attracted by something to have come so close to the villa, for as soon as they were level with it, they wheeled around military fashion to form an extension of the front line of those which, still and motionless with bills buried in their feathers, were riding at anchor, as it were. Only the reeds were gently swaying behind their backs. A long time went by in this way. But at last one of them stationed himself within the immediate proximity of the balcony, craning his neck as though to make an announcement.

"For whom is it meant?" Sander asked. "For the Prince or Dussek or for the sinumbra oil lamp?"[18]

"Naturally for the Prince," Dussek replied.

"And why?"

"Because he isn't only a Prince but also Dussek and *sine umbra*."

They all laughed (including the Prince), while Sander in duly ceremonious fashion offered his congratulations "on the appointment to the post of court musician."

"And when our friend," he concluded, "in future again

gathers straws to find out 'from which direction the wind is blowing,' the wind will always seem to him to be coming from the land of hallowed traditions and no longer from the land of prejudices."

As Sander continued in this vein, the swan flottila, which must have been attracted by Dussek's music, set off again, sailing downstream as they had earlier traveled upstream. Only the swan that had acted as leader appeared once more as if for a renewed offer of thanks and a most formal farewell. Then he, too, shifted to a midstream position and followed in the wake of the others, whose spearhead had already disappeared under the shade of the trees of the park.

VIII

Schach and Victoire

It was shortly after this dinner at the Prince's that it became known in Berlin that the King would be coming over from Potsdam before the end of the week to review the troops at a great parade on Tempelhof Field. News of the occasion this time aroused more than the usual interest, inasmuch as the whole population not only mistrusted the peace terms Haugwitz had brought back, but was also increasingly wedded to the conviction that in the last resort only the country's own strength would prove to be its safeguard or salvation. But what other strength did it command than that of the army, the army which as far as appearance and training were concerned was still that of its Frederickian antecedents?

This was the mood in which the day of the parade, a Saturday, was being anticipated.

The scene the city presented from the early hours corresponded to the prevailing excitement. People poured out by the thousands and were massed in a solid line from Halle Gate all along the ascending highway, on both sides of which the "haversack chaps," those familiar camp followers, had ensconced themselves with their baskets and bottles. Presently, the carriages of the fashionable world appeared, among them Schach's, which had been placed at the disposal of the Carayon ladies for the day. Seated in the carriage with them was an old Herr von der Recke, a former officer, who, as a close relative of Schach's, was doing the honors and at the same time acting as military interpreter. Frau von Carayon was wearing a silk dress of gunmetal gray and a matching cape, while a blue veil covering Victorie's broad-brimmed hat was fluttering in the wind. Beside the coachman sat the groom, pleased with the attention the two ladies were paying him, especially with the rather arbitrarily pronounced words in English that Victoire from time to time addressed to him.

The King's arrival had been announced for eleven o'clock, but the famous old regiments directed to take part in the review, Alt-Larisch, von Arnim, and Möllendorff, appeared long before, preceded by their military bands. They were followed by the cavalry: Garde du Corps, Gensdarmes, and Hussar Body Guard until, at the tail end, the six- and twelve-pounders came clattering and rattling along in an ever denser cloud of dust, some of them veterans of the cannonades of Prague and Leuthen[1] and, more recently, of Valmy and Pirmasens.[2] Their appearance was greeted with enthusiastic cheers and, indeed, to see them approach like this could not fail to make one's heart beat faster in a surge of patriotic pride. The Carayons, too, shared in this general feeling and took it to be mere peevishness or the nervous apprehension of old age when Herr von der Recke, leaning forward and in a voice quivering with emotion, said:

"Let us fix this scene in our memory, ladies, for trust an old man's presentiment, we shan't live to see such splendor again. This is the valedictory parade of the Frederickian army."

Victoire had caught a slight chill on Tempelhof Field and stayed at home when her mother drove to the theater toward evening, a diversion she had always been fond of, never more so than during that season when the artistic presentations on the stage were blended with a refreshing ingredient of political sentiment. *Wallenstein, The Maid of Orleans, William Tell*[3] were occasionally put on, but the play most frequently offered was Holberg's *Political Tinker*,[4] which, as both audience and management may have felt, lent itself rather better to noisy demonstrations than Schiller's muse.

Victoire was alone. The peace and quiet were a welcome relief and, wrapped in a Turkish shawl, she was lying on the sofa, lost in reverie, in front of her a letter she had received just before setting off in the carriage that morning and then only hastily skimmed—to give all the more time and attention to it, of course, upon her return from the parade.

It was a letter from Lisette.

She again took it up and read a passage she had earlier marked with a pencil:

. . . You must understand, my dear Victoire, that I—forgive me for being so blunt—cannot altogether accept some of the things you said in your last letter. You're trying to fool me and yourself when you say you see yourself adopting an attitude of filial devotion towards S. He would smile himself if he heard it. That you should suddenly feel so hurt, no, if you'll excuse me, so piqued when he took the arm of your mama gives you away and makes me wonder about this and a number of other points you mention in this connection. I suddenly come to see a side of you I had not been aware of before, a tendency, in other words, to be suspicious. And now, my dear Victoire, take what I have to say to you on this important point in good part. I'm the older one, you know. You must on no account fall into the habit of harboring suspicion toward those who are definitely entitled to expect the opposite. And I daresay they include Schach. The more I think about the matter, the more I'm driven to the conclusion that you are simply faced with a choice and will have to rid yourself either of the high opinion you have of S. or of your distrust *toward* him. He's a gentleman, you tell me, 'indeed, the chivalrous quality,' you add, was 'the very essence of his make-up,' and in the same breath your suspicion convicts him of a form of behavior which, if it were true, would be the most unchivalrous performance under the sun. You can't have it both ways. Either one is a man of integrity or one isn't. For the rest, my dear Victoire, be assured beyond any shadow of doubt: *the mirror tells you a lie*. There's but *one* thing we women live for, and that is to capture a heart, but *how* we go about it is immaterial.

Victoire folded up the letter again. "Advice and solace are cheap when you're well provided for; she's got everything and now she's being generous. Crumbs of rhetoric dropping off the rich man's table."

And she covered both eyes with her hands.

At that very moment, she heard the doorbell ring, and presently a second time, without any of the servants going to answer it. Had Beate and old Janesch not heard it? Or were they out? Curiosity got the better of her. So she quietly went up to the door and looked out into the vestibule. It was Schach. For a moment she was in some doubt as to what she had better do, but then she opened the glassdoor and asked him to come in.

"You rang so softly. Beate can't have heard it."

"I've only come to inquire how the ladies are. It was perfect weather for a parade, cool and sunny, though there was quite a brisk wind blowing all the same . . ."

"And you see in me one of its victims. I'm feverish, not unduly exactly, but still enough to have had to forgo the theater. The shawl (in which I hope you won't mind my bundling myself up again) and this concoction of herbs, which Beate expects to work outright miracles, are likely to do me more good than *Wallenstein's Death*. Mama wanted to keep me company at first. But you know her passion for everything entitled drama, and so I made her go. Also out of selfishness, of course, for I might as well admit it, I was longing for some peace."

"Which my arrival has now disrupted *after all*. But not for long, only just long enough to deliver a message, to relay a query, with which I may well be coming too late as it is if Alvensleben has already said something."

"Which I don't believe he has, assuming it isn't anything Mama has seen fit to be tight-lipped about even in front of me."

"A very unlikely case, since the message is meant for mother *and* daughter both. We were dining at the Prince's, *cercle intime*,[5] with Dussek needless to say turning up eventually as well. He talked about the theater (what else would he talk about) and managed to reduce even Bülow to silence, which may rank as a feat."

"I declare, dear Schach, you're talking with a spiteful tongue."

"I've been a habitué of Frau von Carayon's salon long enough to have acquired at least the rudiments of this art."

"Getting worse and worse, one heresy outdoing the other. I shall haul you before Mama's grand inquisition. And you shan't escape the torture of a moral sermon at least."

"I couldn't conceive of a more pleasant punishment."

"You take it too lightly . . . Now then, the Prince . . ."

"He would like to see you, *both* of you, mother and daughter. Frau Pauline, who as you may know manages his circle, is to call on you with an invitation."

"With which mother and daughter will consider it a particular honor to comply."

"Which I'm more than a little astonished to hear. And you can't have meant this seriously, my dear Victoire. I find the Prince a gracious lord and have a deep affection for him. No need to waste any words on that. But he's a light with an ocean of shadow or, if you will allow the metaphor, the light smoldering at the charred end of a wick. All in all, he has the dubious distinction of so many royal personages of being equally adept at exploits of war and love, or, to put it more plainly still, he alternates between a prince hero and a prince profligate. At the same time unprincipled and devil-may-care, snapping his fingers even at keeping up appearances. Which may be the worst part of it. You know of his liaison with Frau Pauline?"

"Yes."

"And . . ."

"I don't approve of it. But not to approve of it is not the same as condemning it. Mama has taught me not to concern myself with such matters and not to get wrought up over them. And isn't she right? I ask you, dear Schach, what would become of us, especially of us women, if we set ourselves up as moral judges in our everyday and social surroundings and subjected the lads and lasses to close scrutiny as to the propriety of their actions? Exposing them, say, to an ordeal by water and fire. Society reigns supreme. What it sanctions is legitimate, what it proscribes is beyond the pale. Moreover, this is a special case. The Prince is the Prince, Frau von Carayon is a widow, and I . . . am I."

"And this is to stand as the last word on the matter, Victoire?"

"Yes. The gods balance the scales. And as Lisette Perbandt has just written to me: 'Who's suffered a loss will be compensated in return.' In my case the exchange has been a somewhat bitter pill and I would naturally have preferred to do without it. On the other hand, I'm not blindly ignoring what gains have come my way in exchange and I'm glad of my freedom. What others of my age and sex face with trepidation is open to me. That evening at the Massov ball, where I was for the first time the object of flattering attention, I was, without being aware of it, a slave. Or at any rate subject to a hundred different constraints. Now I'm free."

Schach looked at her in surprise. Some of the things the Prince had said about her were passing through his mind. Had she spoken out of inner conviction or in a sudden access of whim? Was it the fever? Her cheeks were flushed and in the fire flashing in her eyes he caught an expression of defiant resolve. However, he tried to recover the casual tone in which their conversation had begun, saying:

"My dear Victoire is in a playful mood. I bet it's a book by Rousseau that's lying in front of her, and her imagination finds itself in tune with the author."

"No, it's not Rousseau. It's somebody else who interests me *more*."

"And *who* if I may be so bold as to ask?"

"Mirabeau."

"And why *more*?"

"Because I feel a greater affinity for him.[6] And it's always the most subjectively personal that determines how we react. Or almost always, that is. He's my companion, my fellow sufferer par excellence. He grew up showered with adulations. 'Ah, the lovely child,' they kept saying day in and day out. And then one day it was all over, over and done with as . . . as . . ."

"No, Victoire, you're not to say it."

"But I *want* to and would use the name of my companion and fellow sufferer as my own if I could. Victoire *Mirabeau* de Carayon, or rather, Mirabelle de Carayon, that has a natural and felicitous ring, and if I translate it correctly, it means enchantress."

And saying this, she gave a laugh full of exuberance and bitterness, but the tone of bitterness predominated.

"Not *this* kind of laugh, Victoire, you mustn't, not this. It doesn't suit you, it makes you look ugly. Yes, go on, pout—makes you look *ugly*. The Prince was certainly right when he talked about you in such glowing terms. Sterile canon of color and form. The only thing that counts is the one abiding fact that the soul creates its body or shines through it and transfigures it."

Victoire's lips were trembling, her self-assurance gave way, and she was shivering with cold. She pulled her shawl up higher, and Schach took her hand, which was icy, with all her blood rushing toward her heart.

"Victoire, you're not being fair to yourself; you're pointlessly doing violence to yourself and aren't a whit better than those pessimists who have an eye for nothing but the gloomy side of things and fail to see the radiant light of God's sun. I implore you, pull yourself together and think of yourself again as entitled to life and love. Was I blind then? With that bitter word with which you sought to abase yourself, with that very word you summed it up perfectly once and for all. Everything about you radiates an air of fairy tale and enchantment, yes, Mirabelle, yes, enchantress!"

Oh, these were the words her heart had been yearning

for, whereas it had sought to don the armor of defiance.

And now she was listening to them in a daze of silent and blissful abandon.

The clock in the room struck nine and was answered by the church clock outside. Victoire, who had been keeping count of the strikes, smoothed back her hair and stepped up to the window and looked out into the street.

"What are you upset about?"[7]

"I thought I'd heard the carriage."

"You've a too sensitive ear."

But she shook her head, and at that very moment Frau von Carayon's carriage was pulling up.

"Go now . . . Please."

"Until tomorrow."

And without being sure whether he would succeed in avoiding Frau von Carayon, he quickly took his leave and scurried off through the anteroom and corridor.

Everything was quiet and dark, and only a streak of light from the center of the front hall fell within reach of the top flight of the stairs. But he was favored by good luck. A massive pillar almost abutting on to the banisters of the staircase divided the narrow vestibule in two, and he stepped behind the pillar and waited.

Victoire stood in the frame of the glass paneled door and was greeting her mother.

"You're so early. Oh, and how I've been waiting for you."

Schach caught every word. "First the sin, then the lie," said an inner voice. "The old story."

But the barb of his remarks was aimed at himself and not at Victoire.

Then he emerged from his hideout and went quickly and noiselessly down the stairs.

IX

Schach Beats a Retreat

"Until tomorrow," had been Schach's parting words, but he did not come. Nor did he on the second and third day. Victoire tried to puzzle it out and when she couldn't, took up Lisette's letter and kept rereading the passage she had long since come to know by heart. "You must on no account fall into the habit of harboring suspicion toward those who are definitely entitled to expect the opposite. And I daresay they include Schach. The more I think about the matter, the more I'm driven to the conclusion that you are simply faced with a choice and will have to rid yourself either of the high opinion you have of S. or of your distrust *toward* him." Yes, Lisette was right, and yet an anxious feeling lingered in her heart. "If only all the same everything would . . ." And she blushed to the roots of her hair.

At last, on the fourth day he came. But it so happened that she had shortly before gone into town. When she returned she learned of his visit. He was said to have been very gracious, to have inquired after her two or three times, and to have left a bunch of flowers for her. They were violets and roses which pervaded the room with their scent. Victoire, as her mother was regaling her with an account of the visit, made an effort to affect a casual and light-hearted tone, but she was torn by too many conflicting emotions and she withdrew to let her tears born of happiness as much as of foreboding flow unchecked.

Meanwhile the day had come for the performance of *The Consecration of Strength*. Schach sent his man-servant to ask whether the ladies were thinking of going to see it. This was purely a matter of form, since he knew that they would be going.

At the theater, every seat was occupied. Schach sat opposite the Carayons and acknowledged them with a very courteous salutation. But he confined himself to this greeting and did not go over to their box, a reserve at which Frau von Carayon was hardly less taken aback than Victoire. However, the controversy the audience was embroiled in, split as it was into two camps over the play, was so agitated and impassioned that the ladies were carried away as well and, for the time being at least, forgot all personal concerns. Only when they were on their way home did their astonishment at Schach's behavior revive.

The following morning he had himself announced. Frau von Carayon was pleased, but Victoire, more discerning, was filled with profound dismay. He had patently been waiting for this day so as to have a ready-made topic of conversation to fall back on and in this way to smooth over the awkwardness of a first reunion with her. He kissed Frau von Carayon's hand and then turned to Victoire to tell her how sorry he had been to have missed her on his last visit. One was in danger of drifting apart instead of being brought closer together. The way he said this left a doubt in her mind whether his words had a deeper meaning or had merely been spoken out of embarrassment. She fell to pondering it, but before she could think it through the conversation had turned to the play.

"How do you like it?" asked Frau von Carayon.

"I don't care for comedies," Schach replied, "that have a five-hour run. What I look for in the theater is entertainment or diversion, not an ordeal."

"Agreed. But that's an extraneous aspect, a defect, moreover, that's about to be remedied. Iffland himself is agreeable to extensive cutting. I want your opinion of the play."

"It did *not* appeal to me."

"And why not?"

"Because it turns everything upside down. *That* sort of Luther, thank heavens, never existed, and if his like were ever to appear he'd merely take us back to the conditions from which the authentic Luther had rescued us at the time. Every line runs counter to the spirit and century of the Reformation, everything exudes Jesuitism or mysticism and in a frivolous and well-nigh infantile way plays fast and loose with truth and history. Nothing is relevant. I kept being reminded of an engraving by Dürer showing Pilate on horseback with pistol holsters or of an equally well-known work above the altar at Soest in which instead of the paschal lamb a West-phalian ham graces the dish. But what is dished up in this would-be Luther play is the most popish of popish priests. It's an anachronism from beginning to end."

"All right. So much for Luther. But I repeat, the *play*?"

"Luther *is* the play. The rest doesn't count. Or am I to go into raptures over Katharina von Bora,[1] over a nun who after all wasn't one?"

Victoire lowered her eyes, and her hand was trembling. Schach saw it and, alarmed at his blunder, he now spoke hurriedly, his words tumbling over one another, about a skit said to be impending, about a threatened protest by the Lutheran clergy, about the Court, about Iffland, about the playwright himself, ending up with exaggerated praise of the interpolated songs and musical interludes. He hoped Fräulein Victoire remembered the evening on which he had the privilege of accompanying the recital of these songs on the piano.

All this was spoken in a very friendly tone, but for all its friendliness there was also an undertone of constraint, and Victoire with a sensitive ear perceived that it was not *that* talk which she had a right to expect. She tried to reply to him in a free and easy manner, but the conversation continued in a perfunctory vein until he left.

The day after this visit Aunt Marguerite called. She

had heard at Court about the splendid play, "said to be so splendid there'd never been anything like it before," and so she was anxious to see it. Frau von Carayon duly obliged, took her along to see the second performance, and as there had really been a good deal of cutting, there was enough time to spare for half an hour's chit-chat at home.

"Well, Aunt Marguerite," Victoire asked, "how did you like it?"

"Very much, Victoire dear. After all, it touches on the main issue in our purged church."

"What issue are you referring to, Auntie?"

"Why, the one to do with Christian marriage."

Victoire made an effort to keep a straight face and went on:

"I thought the main issue in our church was rather bound up with something else, for instance with the lesson of the Last Supper."

"Oh, no, Victoire dear, *that* I know for certain. Whether it's to be with or without wine—that doesn't make all that difference, but whether the union our married clergy live in is one that was properly solemnized in church or not, *that*, my little angel, is the really important thing."

"And I think Aunt Marguerite is quite right," said Frau von Carayon.

"And it's just that," continued the recipient of this wholly unexpected compliment, "what the play is driving at and what one comes to see all the more clearly, as the actress, Bethmann, is certainly a very good-looking woman. Or at least much better-looking than she actually was—the nun, I mean. Which doesn't matter, since he wasn't a good-looking man either and nowhere near as good-looking as this one. Yes, go on, blush, Victoire dear, I wasn't born yesterday either."

Frau von Carayon was laughing heartily.

"And about this there can be no doubt: our Captain of the Cavalry von Schach must be a *very* genial man, and I keep thinking of Tempelhof and of the Templar standing tall and erect . . . And d'you know, there's supposed to be another one in Wilmersdorf, too, which is also said to be worn smooth like that. And from whom I've got this? Well, from whom d'you think? From *la petite princesse* Charlotte."

X

"Something's Got to Be Done"

The Consecration of Strength was still playing and Berlin continued to be divided into two camps. All those who were mystical-romantic-minded declared *for*, all those who were freethinking, *against* the play. The dispute extended even to the Carayons' ménage, and whereas Mama, partly because of the Court, partly because of her own "feelings," joined in the raving acclaim, Victoire felt repelled by these sentimentalities. She thought it was all false and insincere and maintained that Schach had been absolutely right in everything he had said.

The latter would now pay his visits at sporadic intervals, and then only if he could be sure of finding Victoire in her mother's company. He was again a frequent guest in the "houses of eminence," bestowing, as Nostitz quipped, upon the Radziwills and Carolaths[1] what he was depriving the Carayons of. Alvensleben also made fun of it, and even Victoire tried to strike the same tone, though without managing to bring it off. She spent the days lost in reverie and yet was not really sad, much less unhappy.

Those who took an active interest in the play, that is, in the topic of the day, also included the officers of the Gensdarmes Regiment, even though they did not dream of seriously taking sides either *pro* or *con*. They only had an eye for the comic side of it all and saw in the dissolution of a convent, in Katharina von Bora's nine-year-old foster daughter, and, finally, in the perpetually flute-playing Luther inexhaustible material for their sarcasm and levity.

Their favorite meeting place in those days was the regimental orderly room, where the younger comrades-in-arms would drop in on the duty officer and disport themselves until well into the night. In the discussions they had here about the new comedy the frivolities referred to were hardly ever omitted from the agenda. And when one of the group suggested that it behooved the regiment, which had of late lost some of its former luster, out of a kind of patriotic duty once again to "prove its mettle," he was greeted with a wild outburst of cheers, at the end of which they were all agreed that "something had got to be done." That this could only mean burlesquing *The Consecration of Strength*, for instance by a masquerade, was a foregone conclusion, and the only remaining divergence of views concerned the "how." They therefore decided to have a further meeting in a few days' time at which, after listening to a number of proposals, the appropriate plan would finally be adopted.

The news quickly made the rounds, and the appointed day and hour saw some twenty of the regimental comrades gathered at the above rendezvous: Itzenplitz, Jürgass, and Britzke, Billerbeck, and Diricke, Count Haeseler, Count Herzberg, von Rochow, von Putlitz, a Kracht, a Klitzing, and, last but not least, an already somewhat older Lieutenant von Zieten, an ugly, short, bow-legged little fellow who, as a distant relative of the famous general[2] and perhaps even more by filling the air with the impudent luster of his rasping voice, contrived to make up for what other virtues he lacked. Nostitz and Alvensleben had also appeared. Schach was absent.

"Who's going to take the chair?" Klitzing asked.

"Only two possibilities," Diricke replied. "The tallest or the shortest. In other words, Nostitz or Zieten."

"Nostitz, Nostitz," they all cried in a babel of voices, and the winner of this election by acclamation sat down in a dented garden chair. There were bottles and glasses covering the entire length of the long table.

"Speech! *Assemblée nationale . . .*"

Nostitz allowed the hubbub to continue for a while before rapping on the table with the broadsword lying by his side as his badge of office.

"Silence, silence."

"Brother officers of the Gensdarmes Regiment, heirs to an ancient glory in the realm of military and social honor (for we haven't only set the trend in combat, we've also set the *fashion* in society). Brother officers, I say, we have resolved: *something's got to be done!*"

"Yes, yes. Something's got to be done."

"And consecrated anew through *The Consecration of Strength*, we have decided, for old Luther's and our own benefit, to organize a procession, which shall be talked of through the ages down to the last generation. It calls for something on the grand scale! Let us remember that he who doesn't move forward slips back. A procession then. That part is settled. But type and makeup of this procession remain to be decided, and it's for this that we're met here. I'm ready to listen to your suggestions one by one. Whoever has any suggestions to make put up his hand."

Those who did so included Lieutenant von Zieten.

The latter got up, and seesawing gently, hands on the back of his chair, said:

"What I've in mind is known as *sleigh ride*."

They all looked at each other, some of them laughing. "In July?"

"In July," Zieten returned. "Sprinkle some salt along Unter den Linden and there's snow for you to speed you on your ride. First, a few hysterical nuns, but in the big main sleigh forming the center of the procession, Luther and his famulus are on view, each complete with flute, while Katie is perched on the box, either with a torch or horsewhip, according to taste. Outriders to lead off the procession. Costumes will be requisitioned from the theater or specially made. I've spoken."

A deafening upraor was the reply until Nostitz, calling for order, eventually prevailed.

"I simply take this hullabaloo to mean that everybody

agrees, and want to congratulate our comrade von
Zieten for immediately scoring a bull's eye with a single
and opening expert shot. Sleigh ride it is. Motion
adopted?"

"Yes, yes."

"All that remains is to name the cast. Who's going to
play Luther?"

"Schach."

"He'll refuse."

"Not so," crowed Zieten, who harbored a special
grudge against handsome Schach, in whose favor he had
on more than one occasion been passed over. "How can
anyone so badly misjudge Schach! I know him better.
No doubt he'll grumble for half an hour at having to
clap on high cheekbones and to convert his normal oval
shape into a clodhopper's squarehead. But he'll end up
by matching vanity with vanity and getting a thrill out
of the prospect of being for twenty-four hours the one-
day man of destiny."

Before Zieten had finished, a corporal arrived from
the guard to deliver a message addressed to Nostitz.

"Ah, *lupus in fabula*."[3]

"From Schach?"

"Yes!"

"Read, read!"

And Nostitz tore open the letter and read.

"I would appreciate it, dear Nostitz, if at the meeting
of our young officers, which is presumably taking place
as I write, you would act as my spokesman and, if neces-
sary, also as my advocate. I have received the circular

and had at first been willing to come. But I have since been told what the meeting is likely to be about, and this information has made me change my mind. It will be no secret to you that all that's being planned goes against my conviction so that you can easily calculate how much or how little I (for whom even a Luther on the stage went against the grain) care for a Luther in a masquerade. That we're going to have this masquerade take place in a period that cannot claim license even for a carnival certainly doesn't help. At the same time, my attitude in this matter is not meant to exert any pressure on the younger of our comrades, and in any event I can be relied on for strictest confidence. I'm not the Regiment's conscience, much less its keeper. Yours, Schach."

"I knew it," Nostitz said with perfect calm, burning Schach's note in the nearest candleflame. "Friend Zieten's is better at projects and fantasies than at judging human nature. He wants to answer me back, I see, but I'm not free to oblige him, since at this moment all we're concerned with is: who's going to play Luther? I'm putting the Reformer under the hammer. He goes to the highest bidder. Going . . . going . . . gone. Nobody? Then all I can do is nominate somebody. Alvensleben, you."

The latter shook his head. "I feel about it like Schach. Have your fun. I'm no spoilsport, but personally I'm not going to be a party to it. Can't and won't. There's too much Lutheran catechism in my bones for that."

Nostitz was not immediately prepared to yield.

"There's a time and place for everything," he said,

"and if one's to be serious for a day, one may surely have fun for an hour. You're too moralistic, too solemn, too rigid about everything. That, too, is like Schach. There's nothing either good or bad as such. Remember we aren't out to parody old Luther, on the contrary, we want to vindicate him. What we do mean to parody is the *play*, is the caricature of Luther, the Reformer presented in a false light and a wrong setting. We're a tribunal, a court of the very highest standard of ethics. Join us. You mustn't leave us in the lurch or else everything will go by the board."

Others spoke in the same vein. But Alvensleben stood his ground, and an air of slight ill-feeling was dispelled only when young Count Herzberg unexpectedly (and for that very reason greeted with the most widespread cheers) got up to volunteer for the part of Luther.

All the remaining details were speedily disposed of, and in less than ten minutes the major roles had been assigned: Count Herzberg as Luther; Diricke as famulus; Nostitz, because of his enormous height, as Katharina von Bora. The others were simply listed as so many nuns, and only Zieten, to whom they felt specially indebted, was promoted to abbess. He promptly served notice that he was going to "try his hand at a game" in his seat in the sleigh or play a game of *mariage* with the abbot. This was met by another outburst of cheers, and after Monday had quickly been fixed as the day for the masquerade, and the most stringent ban been imposed on any blabbing, Nostitz closed the meeting.

In the door Diricke turned around once more, asking:

"What if it rains?"

"It *mustn't* rain."

"And what about the salt?"

"*C'est pour les domestiques!*"

"*Et pour la canaille*,"[4] concluded the youngest cornet.

XI

The Sleigh Ride

Secrecy had been sworn, and the secret was really kept. A case without parallel perhaps. True enough, it was being bruited about in town that the Gensdarmes had "something up their sleeve" and were once again hatching one of those mad pranks for which they had a reputation that exceeded that of other regiments, but there was no indication as to what the madness was going to involve or for what day it had been planned. Even the Carayon ladies, at whose last soirée neither Schach nor Alvensleben had appeared, had been left in the dark so that the famous "summer sleigh ride" took those more immediately and those less immediately concerned equally by surprise.

One of the stables in the vicinity of Mittel- and Dorotheenstrasse served as the point of assembly at dusk. On the stroke of nine, preceded by a dozen sumptuously attired horse guards and flanked by torch-bearers, in other words, just as Zieten had suggested, the cavalcade shot past the Academy building toward the Linden, swept, further down, first into the Wilhelmstrasse but then, doubling back, into the Behren- and Charlottenstrasse and once more circled the Linden square just mentioned at an ever accelerating pace.

When the cavalcade passed the Carayons' house the *first* time and all the windowpanes of the *bel étage*[1] were caught in the glare of the torches of the riders in the advance column, Frau von Carayon, who happened to be alone, rushed to the window in alarm and looked out into the street. But instead of hearing the cry of "fire" she had expected, all she heard, as in the depth of winter, was a cracking of hunters' and sleigh drivers' whips with jingling bells in between, and before she could make out what was going on, it had all flashed past, leaving her bewildered and perplexed and half dazed. This was the state she was in when Victoire found her.

"For heaven's sake, Mama, what's the matter?"

But before Frau von Carayon was able to reply, the spearhead of the cavalcade had appeared a *second* time, and mother and daughter, having quickly, for closer scrutiny, stepped from their corner room out to the balcony, were no longer in any doubt about the meaning of it all. Mockery, whoever or whatever the target in question. First, some lewd nuns, with a witch of an abbess in the lead, yelling, drinking, playing cards, and in the middle of the procession the main sleigh running on casters and with its profuse gold trimmings clearly meant as the triumphal car in which Luther and his famulus and, on the box, Katharina von Bora were sitting. By the tall figure they recognized Nostitz. But who was that in the front seat? Victoire was wondering. Who was hiding behind the mask of Luther? *He*, was it? No, it couldn't be. And yet, even if it wasn't, he was implicated in this revolting spectacle all the same, having approved of it or at any rate done nothing to prevent it. What a corrupt world it was, how frivolous, how utterly lacking in decency! How vacuous and sickening. It pained her beyond words to see the beautiful being perverted and the virtuous dragged in the mud. And what was it all for? To be in the limelight for a day, to gratify some petty vanity. And *that* was the world in which she had dwelt with her reveries and laughter, that had come to be the very warp and woof of her life, that had made her yearn for love and, alas, worst of all, believe in love!

"Let's go," she said, taking her mother's arm, and turned to go back into the room. But before she could get to it, she was overcome as though she were going to faint and collapsed on the doorstep of the balcony.

Her mother pulled the bell rope, Beate came in and together they carried her to the sofa, where she was immediately seized by severe spasms in her chest. She burst into sobs, sat up, fell back onto the pillows, and when her mother wanted to dab her forehead and temples with eau de cologne she angrily pushed her back. But the next moment she snatched the flask out of her mother's hand and was dousing her shoulders and neck.

"I hate myself, hate myself as I do the world. When I was ill that time I begged God to save my life . . . But we *ought* not to beg for our life . . . God knows best what's good for us. And if He means to call us to Him we ought not to beg: grant us yet . . . Oh, how painfully it's being borne in on me! I live, yes . . . But how, how!"

Frau von Carayon knelt down beside the sofa and was talking to her. But at that very moment the cavalcade charged past the house a *third* time and again it seemed as though in the red glow of the reflection the black shapes of imaginary figures were caught up in a game of touch-and-run.

"Doesn't it remind you of hell?" Victoire said, pointing to the phantasmagoria of shadows on the ceiling.

Frau von Carayon sent Beate to ask the doctor to come. But actually she was interested less in the doctor than in their being alone and in having a heart-to-heart talk with the poor girl.

"What's the matter with you? And heavens, how you're shaking and trembling all over. I no longer recognize my gay Victoire. Look at it calmly, child, what has happened after all? Another mad prank, one of many, and I remember times when you would have laughed at, rather than shed tears over, such antics. It's something else that's worrying and depressing you; I've been noticing it for days. But you're concealing it from me, you're nursing a secret. I implore you, Victoire, tell me. There's nothing to be afraid of. It doesn't matter, whatever it is."

Victoire flung her arms around Frau von Carayon's neck, and her eyes were streaming with tears.

"Mother dearest."

And she pulled her closer and kissed her and made a clean breast of everything.

XII

Schach at Frau von Carayon's

The following morning Frau von Carayon was seated at her daughter's bedside, saying as the latter looked up at her affectionately and with an air of newly regained calm and happiness:

"Take heart, child. I've known him for such a long time. He's weak and vain like all good-looking men, but with no ordinary sense of fair play and an unimpeachable integrity."

At that moment Captain of the Cavalry von Schach was announced, old Jannasch adding that he had shown him into the drawing room.

Frau von Carayon nodded approvingly.

"I knew he'd come," said Victoire.

"Because you dreamed it?"

"No, not dreamed. I just observe and put two and two together. For some time now I've been able to tell in advance on which day and under what circumstances he's liable to turn up. He always comes when there's some public event or a piece of news on which he can conveniently seize as a topic of conversation. He steers clear of any talk of a personal nature with me. That's how he came after the performance of the play and today he comes after the performance of the sleigh ride. I do wonder if he had anything to do with it. If so, tell him how much I was put out by it. Or perhaps you'd better not."

Frau von Carayon was moved. "Oh, Victoire, my sweet, you're too good, much too good. He doesn't deserve it, no one does." And patting her daughter, she crossed the corridor into the drawing room, where Schach was waiting for her.

He seemed less inhibited than he usually was and, bowing, kissed her hand, to which she graciously submitted. And yet her manner seemed different. She indicated with unwonted formality one of the Japanese chairs standing to the side, pushed a hassock into place for her feet and herself sat down on the sofa.

"I've come to inquire how the ladies are and whether the masquerade yesterday met with approval or not."

"Frankly, it didn't. Speaking for myself, I thought it was hardly in good taste, and its effect on Victoire bordered on disgust."

"A sentiment I share."

"Then you had no part in it?"

"Certainly not. And I'm surprised I still have to be expilcit about it at this point. You know, don't you, where I stand on this question, my dear Josephine, have known it ever since that evening when we first talked about the play and its author. What I said then still holds today. Serious themes also call for serious treatment, and I'm genuinely pleased to see that Victoire is on my side. Is she in?"

"In bed."

"Nothing serious, I hope."

"Yes and no. The after-effects of spasms in her chest and of a fit of weeping that came upon her last night."

"No doubt as a result of that buffoonery of a masquerade. I'm deeply sorry to hear it."

"And yet I owe that buffoonery a debt of gratitude. Her disgust with that masquerade business, of which she was an involuntary witness, loosened her tongue. She broke her long silence and confided a secret to me, a secret you know."

Schach, feeling doubly guilty, blushed to the roots of his hair.

"Dear Schach," Frau von Carayon continued, taking his hand and fixing her intelligent eyes on him with a friendly but firm look, "dear Schach, I'm not such a ninny as to subject you to a scene, let alone a sermon on morality. The things I detest most include self-righteous homilies. I've been exposed to the ways of the world since my youth, know it for what it is, and have had my own fair share of personal experience. And even if I were hypocrite enough to want to conceal it from myself and others, how could I do so from *you?*"

She paused for a minute, dabbing her forehead with her cambric handkerchief. Then she continued by way of amplification:

"Of course, there are those, and especially among us women, who interpret the saying about the left hand supposedly not knowing what the right hand is doing to the effect that today supposedly doesn't know of yesterday's doings. Not to mention those of the day before yesterday! But I don't belong to those feminine adepts at lapses of memory. I don't delude myself about anything, refuse to, it's not my way. And now rebuke me if you can."

He was visibly affected as she kept talking like this, and his whole manner showed what a hold she still had over him.

"Dear Schach," she went on, "you see I put myself at the mercy of your judgment. But even though I unreservedly refrain from upholding or championing the cause of Josephine (forgive me, but you have yourself just now invoked the old name again), I cannot afford to forgo being the advocate of *Frau* von Carayon, of her house and her name."

Schach seemed about to interrupt, but she would not let him.

"Another minute. I'm practically done with what I want to say. Victoire has asked me to hush up *everything*, not to breathe a word to anyone, not even to *you*, and not to demand amends. In order to expiate half an offense (and it's putting it high when I say *half*) she wants to shoulder *all* of it, even toward the outside world, and with that romantic streak peculiar to her make her misfortune grow into a good fortune. She glories in the high-minded feeling of self-abnegation, out of a sweet surrender for the sake of *him* who has

won her love and for *that* to which she is *going* to give
her love. But however compliant I may be in my love for
Victoire, I'm not compliant enough to fall in with this
quixotic exercise in generosity. I'm a member of a society by whose code I abide, to whose laws I submit;
that was how I was brought up, and I'm not disposed
because of some fanciful notion of sacrifice on my be-
loved darling daughter's part to sacrifice my social position into the bargain as well. In other words, I have no
desire to go into a convent or to assume the ascetic role
of a pillar saint, not even for Victoire's sake. And so I
must insist that the incident in question be duly legiti-
mized. This, Captain, sir, is what I've had to say to you."

Schach, who had meanwhile had a chance to collect
himself, replied that he was well aware that every action
in life brought its logical consequence in its train. And
he had no intention of evading such a consequence. If
he had known before what he had learned now he
would of his own accord have suggested the very steps
that Frau von Carayon was demanding. He had wanted
to remain single, and to dismiss such a long-held idea
from his mind was momentarily causing a certain bewilderment. But he felt no less certain that he would
have reason to congratulate himself on the day that was
shortly to usher in this change in his life. Victoire was
her mother's daughter, which offered the best assurance
for his future, the promise of true happiness.

All this was said in a very courteous and obliging
tone, though at the same time with a notable detachment.

Frau von Carayon felt this in a way that was to her not only wounding but positively offensive. What she had listened to was the language neither of love nor of remorse, and when Schach had fallen silent she caustically replied:

"I'm much obliged for your remarks, Herr von Schach, most especially for those directed at my person. That your 'yes' might have had a more unconstrained and unforced ring you probably realize yourself in your heart of hearts. But never mind, I'm content to accept your 'yes.' For what is it I long for when all is said and done? A marriage service in the Cathedral and a gala wedding. I want to see myself dressed in yellow satin once more, and then when we've had our torchlight dance and the cutting of Victoire's garter[1]—since we'll no doubt have to observe to some extent the style prescribed for a princess, if only because of Aunt Marguerite—why, then I'll give you carte blanche, you'll be free again, as free as a bird in open season, in all your comings and goings, in hate and love, for then after all the step will have been taken that needs *had* to be taken."

Schach made no reply.

"For the time being I proceed on the basis of a tacit engagement. About everything else we shall reach agreement readily enough. If need be, in writing. But the patient is waiting for me, so you must excuse me."

Frau von Carayon got up, and Schach thereupon promptly took his leave with all due formality and without another word having passed between them.

XIII

"Le Choix Du Schach"

They had parted in almost open hostility. But everything went more smoothly than could have been expected after this tense interview, thanks largely to a letter Schach had written to Frau von Carayon a day or
two before. In it, he unreservedly pleaded guilty, pre-
tending, as he had already done in the interview itself,
to surprise and bewilderment and managing to find for
all these declarations a more cordial tone and more
warmhearted words. Indeed, his sense of rectitude,
which he was anxious to gratify, made him perhaps say
more than was prudent and wise. He spoke of his love
for Victoire and, whether by design or by accident,
fought shy of all those professions of esteem and appreciation which are so deeply hurtful when what is
required is a simple avowal of affection. Victoire drank
in every word and her mother, finally putting the letter
aside, saw, not without emotion, how two minutes' hap-

piness had been enough to restore hope in her poor child and, together with this hope, her old gaiety. The patient was radiant, felt as though cured, and Frau von Carayon said:

"How pretty you are, Victoire."

Schach on the very same day received a note in reply telling him openly of his old friend's intense delight. She would ask him to forget some harsh things she had said; impulsive as she was, she had allowed herself to be carried away. For the rest nothing serious and irretrievable had been lost, and if joy proverbially was the seedbed of sorrow, the reverse no doubt also applied. She was again looking forward to the future with confidence and again able to take heart. The personal sacrifice she was making she was glad to make if this sacrifice was indispensable for her daughter's happiness.

Schach, after reading the note, kept pondering it from all angles and was visibly torn in his reaction. He had when speaking of Victoire in his letter given way to an access of kindly-affectionate feeling, such as no one would easily have withheld from her, and had expressed this feeling (he remembered this) with particular fervor. But what the note of his friend was now reminding him of anew went *beyond* this, that simply meant marriage, wedlock, words the mere sound of which had from time immemorial terrified him. Marriage! And marriage with *whom*? With a beauty who, as the Prince had chosen to put it, "had passed through purgatory."

"But," he continued his monologue, "I don't share the Prince's point of view, I don't care for 'purgatorial pro-cesses' about which one can't be sure whether the loss may not exceed the gain, and even if I personally might be converted to this point of view, I certainly couldn't convert the world . . . I'm hopelessly at the mercy of my brother officers' taunts and jibes, and the caricature of a serenely happy 'country marriage' which, violet-like, blooms in hidden seclusion stares me in the face as a veritable model of perfection. I can see exactly how things are going to develop: I resign from the service, take charge of Wuthenow again, work the land, improve the soil, grow rapeseed or turnips, and tread the path of strictest marital fidelity. What a life, what a future! *One* Sunday a sermon; *another*, the gospel or epistles, and in between a game of whist for three, always with the same parson. And then one day, some Prince turns up in the nearest town, perhaps Prince Louis himself, changing horses, while I've gone off to dance attendance on him at the gate or the inn. And subjecting me and my anti-quated coat to searching scrutiny, he inquires how I'm getting on. And all the time his every look proclaims: 'What a difference three years can make in a man.' Three years . . . And perhaps it'll be thirty."

He had been pacing up and down in his room and pausing in front of a pier table on which lay the letter he had put down in the course of his soliloquy. Twice, three times he took it up and dropped it again. "My destiny. Yes, 'the crucial moment determines the choice.' I can still remember that's what she wrote at the time. Did she realize what would happen? Was she *out* for it? Oh, shame on you, Schach, what a slur on the sweet girl!

You're the one who's the guilty party in this. Your *guilt* is your destiny. And I'm willing to let it be on my head."

He rang the bell, gave the servant some instructions, and went off to the Carayons.

It was as if through the monologue he had rid himself of the oppression that had been weighing on him. The tone in which he addressed his old friend was now natural, almost affectionate, and without even the smallest cloud to cast a shadow on Frau von Carayon's newly regained trust, the two of them discussed what arrangements had to be made. Schach showed himself agreeable to everything: in a week's time, the engagement and three weeks later, the wedding. But immediately after the wedding the young couple were to go on a journey to Italy and not to return to their own country for a year, Schach to the capital, Victoire to Wuthenow, the old family estate, of which she retained grateful and pleasant memories from a previous visit (when Schach's mother was still alive). And although the estate had since been leased, the *château* was still there, entirely at their disposal and ready to be moved into at any time.

After settling such matters as these they separated. The sun was smiling on the house of Carayon, and Victoire forgot all about the gloom that had preceded it.

Schach also took stock. To see Italy again had been his ardent wish ever since his first visit there only a few years before; *this* was now to come true. And once they were back they would have no difficulty in deriving a good deal of advantage and benefit also from the two domestic establishments they were contemplating. Vic-

toire loved a life of rural simplicity and peace. Then he
would take leave from time to time and drive or ride
over to Wuthenow. And then they would roam the fields,
chatting away. Oh, she was so good at chatting and
was natural and spirited at the same time. And after yet
another year, or two or three, why, it would all have
blown over, be dead and buried. The world is so quick
to forget and society even more so. And then they'd
move into the corner house in the Wilhelmsplatz, both
of them glad to be living once more under conditions
that meant home after all not only to him but also to
her. It would all have been weathered, and the ship of
life would not have foundered on the rock of ridicule.

Poor Schach. The stars had a different fate in store for
him.

The week that was to pass before the announcement
of the engagement was not yet over when a letter was
sent to him at home addressed in his full title and bearing a large red seal. His first thought was that it was an
official communication (perhaps an appointment to
some post) and he delayed opening it so as not to de-
tract from the joy of anticipation. But where did it come
from? From whom? He examined the seal with curiosity
and now saw plainly enough that it wasn't a seal at all
but the impression of a carved gem. How odd. And now
he opened it, and an illustration tumbled out at him, a
soft-ground etching, with a caption at the bottom: "*Le
choix du* Schach." He repeated the description to himself without being able to make head or tail of it or of
the illustration and only sensed in a very general and

indefinite kind of way an undercurrent of provocation and danger. And in point of fact, having recovered his bearings, he saw that his first reaction had been correct. Enthroned under a canopy sat a Persian Schach, recognizable by his tall lambskin cap, while two female figures were standing at the throne's bottom rung, waiting for the moment when he who was gazing down from his lofty heights with icy and imperious stare would have chosen between them. The Persian Schach, though, was simply *our* Schach, a likeness, that is, drawn with most uncanny fidelity, while the heads of the two ladies eyeing him with questioning glance and sketched in much more impromptu fashion were nonetheless sufficiently close to be easily recognizable as Frau von Carayon and Victoire. In other words, a caricature pure and simple. His relationship with the Carayons had become a subject of gossip in town, and one of his envious fellows and enemies, of whom he had only too many, had seized on the occasion to vent his malicious spleen.

Schach trembled with humiliation and rage, the blood rushed to his head, and he felt stunned beyond words.

Yielding to a natural urge for some air and physical exercise or perhaps also animated by a hunch that his bolt had not yet been shot, he took his hat and sword to go out for a walk. Meeting people and talking to them would provide a diversion and restore his composure. What did it amount to after all? A petty act of vindictiveness.

The fresh air buoyed him up; he breathed more easily and had almost regained his good humor when, turning from the direction of the Wilhelmsplatz into the Linden, he crossed over to the shadier side of the street to greet some acquaintances who were passing that way. But they avoided a conversation and became visibly embarrassed. Zieten, too, appeared on the scene, gave a perfunctory salute and, what's more, if one could believe one's eyes, with a sardonic sneer. Schach gazed after him, wondering about it and trying to decide what the smugness of the one and the embarrassed expressions of the others might mean when he noticed, some hundred paces further on, an unusually large crowd gathered in front of a small picture shop. Some were laughing, others chattering, but all of them seemed to be asking "what it was really all about." Schach skirted round the throng of sightseers, glanced over their heads and saw enough. In the center window hung the identical caricature, the purposely reduced price marked prominently underneath in red crayon.

In other words, a conspiracy.

Schach no longer had the energy to continue his walk and returned to his lodgings.

Around noon Sander received a note from Bülow:

Dear Sander:

I have just been sent a cartoon showing Schach and the Carayon ladies. Not knowing whether you have seen it yet, I'm enclosing it. Please try to track down the source. You're always informed about everything and have your ear to the ground in Berlin. For my part I'm shocked. *Not* because of

Schach, whom this 'Persian' cap fits rather well (for he's really the type for that sort of thing), but because of the Carayons. The genial Victoire! To be pilloried like that. We ape all the worst traits of the French and ignore their good ones, which also includes courtesy.

Yours,
B.

Sander, after no more than a cursory glance at the drawing, with which he was familiar, sat down at his desk and replied:

Mon Général:

There is no need for me to track down the source, it has tracked *me* down. About four or five days ago, a gentleman called at my office and asked me if I would be agreeable to arrange for the distribution of some drawings. When I saw what it was all about I refused. There were three sheets, among them '*Le Choix du* Schach.' The gentleman who called on me passed himself off as a foreigner, but for all his feigned broken German, he spoke it so well that I could not help taking his foreign ways for a mere pose. Some people in the entourage of Prince R. resent our man's flirtations with the Princess and are probably behind all this. But if I'm wrong in this conjecture, one cannot but conclude with something like certainty that it was his comrades in the Regiment. If there's one thing he's not, it's popular; he who affects to be made of different clay never is. One might let the matter pass if it weren't for the fact, as you very rightly point out, that the Carayons have been dragged into this as well. It's because of *them* that I deplore this prank, the malice of which will hardly have run its course with this *one* cartoon. The two others I mentioned above will no doubt turn up in due course. Everything in this anonymous campaign has been cleverly planned, and what has also been cleverly planned is the idea not to administer the poison all at once. It won't fail to have its effect, all that remains to be seen is the 'how.'

Tout à vous,

S.

As a matter of fact, the concern that Sander had expressed in his letter to Bülow was to prove only too well founded. The two other cartoons, intermittently like fever at two-day intervals, also appeared and were, like the first one, bought or at any rate gaped at and discussed by every passer-by. The case Schach-Carayon had become a *cause célèbre* overnight, although the prying public had only a vague idea of what was going on. Schach, they said, had turned his back on the attractive mother and concentrated on the unattractive daughter. The motive was the subject of a good deal of speculation without anyone hitting upon the truth.

Schach received the two other cartoons in an envelope also. The seal was the same as before. Cartoon number two bore the legend, "*La gazza ladra*," or "The Thievish *Schach*-Magpie," and showed a magpie examining two rings that differed in value and picking the more unpretentious one out of a bowl of jewels.

But by far the most offensive was the third cartoon, which had Frau von Carayon's drawing room as a setting. On top of the table stood a chessboard on which, much as after a lost game and as though sealing their doom, the chessmen had been overturned. Victoire, a good likeness, was siting beside it, and Schach, again in the Persian cap of the earlier drawing, was kneeling at her feet. But this time the cap had a tassel and was crumpled. And the caption underneath read: "Schach—checkmate."

These repeated attacks achieved their object only too well. Schach sent word that he was ill, he would see no one, and requested leave, which his commanding officer, Colonel von Schwerin, readily granted him.

So it came about that on the very day on which, by mutual agreement, his engagement to Victoire was to have been announced he left Berlin. He went to his estate without having said goodbye to the Carayons (in whose house he had not set foot during this entire period).

XIV

At Wuthenow on the Lake

It was striking midnight when Schach arrived in Wuthenow, on the far side of which, built on a hill, stood Château Wuthenow which to the right and left commanded a view across Lake Ruppin. In the houses and cottages everything had long been fast asleep, and only from the direction of the stables could one still hear the pawing of a horse or the muffled lowing of a cow.

Schach passed through the village and when he had come to the end, turned into a narrow country lane which, by a gradual ascent, led to the hill of the château. On the right were the trees of the outer grounds, on the left, a freshly mown field, the smell of hay pervading the air. But the château itself was merely a building of whitewashed timberwork inlaid with black-tarred beams. Its utterly monotonous commonplace look had only been disposed of by Schach's mother, her "late ladyship," through the addition of a gable roof, a light-

ning rod, and a magnificent terrace designed on the
model of Sans Souci.[1] Just now, of course, under the
starlit sky, it all suggested a castle in a fairy tale, and
Schach frequently stopped, looking up at it, obviously
affected by the beauty of the scene.

Finally, he arrived at the top and rode up to the entrance gate which formed a low arch between the gable
of the château and an adjoining servants' lodge. From
the courtyard at that moment he caught the sounds of
barking and snarling and heard how the dog in a fury
came bolting out of his kennel and with his chain was
scraping to the right and the left along the wooden
walls.

"Lie down, Hector!"

And the dog, recognizing his master's voice, started to
howl and whine with joy and by turns to jump up and
down from the kennel.

In front of the servants' lodge stood a walnut tree
spreading its branches. Schach dismounted, looped the
reins around the branch and knocked lightly on one of
the shutters. But only after he had tapped again did
anything begin to stir inside, and a voice still drowsy
with sleep reached him from the alcove:

"What's up?"

"It's me, Krist."

"Why, mother, it's the young master."

"Yes, that's him. Better get up and hurry."

Schach could hear every word and good-naturedly
called into the room as he half opened the shutter that
had only been pushed to, "Take your time, old man."

But the old man was already out of bed and kept saying, while searching all over for something: "Coming, young master, coming. I'll only be a minute."

And indeed, it was not long before Schach saw the burning of a sulfurated match and heard the flap of a lantern being snapped open and shut. There it was, a first glint of light flashing through the windowpanes and a pair of wooden clogs clattering along the earthen corridor. And now the bolt was being pushed back, and Krist, who had quickly slipped on some cotton trousers, was standing before his young master. Many a long year ago when his "old lordship" had died and this title born of reverence and respect went begging upon his death, he had wanted to transfer it to his young master. But the latter, who had shot his first coot with Krist and first gone on the lake in the boat with him, would not hear of the new title.

"Why, young master, you'd always first drop us a line or send up a batman or the little English chap. And this time not a peep. But I had such a feeling when the frogs wouldn't be done croaking tonight. 'Mark my word, mother,' says I, 'that means somethin'.' But you know what womenfolk are like. What does she say? 'What's it supposed to mean?' says she. 'Rain, that's what it means. And a good thing too. Because our p'tatoes need it.'"

"Yes, indeed," said Schach, who had been listening with only one ear while the old man was unlocking the door which opened into the château from the gable end. "Yes, indeed. Rain is a good thing. Now just go on ahead."

Krist did as his young master had asked, and they both went down a narrow, tiled passageway. It only widened in the center, forming, on the left, a large vestibule, while on the right French doors profusely decorated with ledges in gilt and rococo work opened into a garden room which had been used by the General's late wife, Frau von Schach, a very distinguished and very dignified old lady, as a living and reception room. It was there the two of them were heading, and when Krist, not without some difficulty and effort, had opened the door, which was considerably warped, they entered.

The large variety of *objets d'art* and mementos which stood about in this garden room included a double candlestick of bronze, which Schach himself, only three years before, had brought back from Italy as a present for his mother. Krist now took it down from the mantelpiece, lit the two candles, which, in their cupped holders, were relics from the days when her late ladyship had used them for sealing her letters. Her ladyship herself, though, had been dead for only a year, and as Schach had not been back here since, everything had been kept in its former place. A few settees were in their old position facing each other along the shorter walls, while two sofas took up the middle of the longer wall, with only the gilt-laid French rococo doors in between. The position of the round rosewood table (an object of the old lady's pride) and of the large marble fruit dish filled with alabaster grapes and oranges and a pineapple had also remained unchanged. But the whole room,

which had not been aired for ages, felt oppressively
stuffy and close.

"Open a window," said Schach. "And let me have a
blanket. That one."

"D'you want to lie down *here* then, young master?"

"Yes, Krist, I do. I've lain in worse places."

"I know. Why, the stories his old lordship used to tell
us about *that*! Always—splash!—right into the muddy
lime. No, no, wouldn't be nothin' for me. 'Why, your
lordship,' I'd always say, 'seems to me he's goin' to be
skinned alive.' But his old lordship just laughed and
said: 'No, Krist, *our* skin's tightly sewn on.' "

While the old man was talking in this vein and recall-
ing the past, he reached all the same for a caned carpet
beater in a corner by the fireplace and tried to remove
the worst from the sofa that Schach had chosen for a
bed. But the dense cloud of dust that rose up showed
the futility of any such efforts, and Schach said with a
touch of good humor:

"Let the dust rest in peace."

And only when the words were out of his mouth was
there double meaning borne in on him, and he thought
of his parents in their large copper coffins with the sol-
dered crucifix which were reposing in the parish church
in the village down below in the old family vault.

But he did not pursue the vision of this scene and
flung himself down on the sofa.

"Give that white horse of mine a crust of bread and a
bucket of water: that'll see him through until tomorrow.
And now put the light on the window sill and leave it

burning . . . No, not there, not in the open window, the one next to it. And now good night, Krist. And lock up from outside so that they won't carry me off."

"Eh, they're not goin' to for sure . . ."

And presently Schach heard the clattering of the clogs receding down the passageway. But even before Krist could have got to the gable entrance and locked up from outside, a pressure, heavy and leaden, had settled on his master's overwrought brain.

But not for long. For all the burden that was oppressing him he became distinctly aware of something buzzing above his head, something brushing and tickling him, and then tossing and turning and even an instinctive and drowsy thrashing about with his hand had no effect, he finally heaved himself up and forced himself to become fully awake again. And now he saw what it was. The two smoldering candlelights just going out, whose smoke had made the already airless room more airless still, had attracted all sorts of winged creatures from the garden, but of what kind and description they were was not yet clear. For a moment he thought they were bats, but presently it was brought home to him that they were merely huge butterflies and moths which were flying about in the room by the dozen and bouncing against the windowpanes in vain attempts to find the open window again.

Seizing the bedclothes, he hit out repeatedly to chase the intruders out of the room again. But the bugs, which as a result of all this chasing and thrashing were only becoming ever more frightened, appeared to be dou-

bling in number and kept buzzing about him in denser
and noisier swarms than before. Any further thought of
sleep was out of the question, and he went up to the
open window and jumped out to await the dawn, strol-
ling about outdoors.

He looked at the clock. Half-past one. The landscaped
grounds directly in front of the garden room consisted of
a round flower bed, complete with sun dial, around
which, in predominantly triangular beds and bordered
by box trees, a variety of summer flowers were in bloom:
mignonettes, larkspurs, lilies, and stock. One could easily tell that there had been no tending hand at work here
of late, even though Krist included gardening among his
multifarious duties. It was, on the other hand, still much
too soon since her ladyship's death for everything to
have gone completely to seed. So far it had only taken
on the form of overgrown lushness, and a heavy and yet
delicious scent of gillyflowers rose from the beds, which
Schach inhaled in ever more eager drafts.

He walked round the flower beds, once, ten times, and
setting one foot in front of the other, picked his way
along the footpaths that were no wider than a hand's
breadth. In this way he meant to test his agility and to
while away the time with good grace. But the time
would not pass, and when he glanced again at the clock,
only a quarter of an hour had gone by.

He abandoned the flowers and went toward one of the
two pergolas that ran along both sides of the spacious
grounds and all the way from the top to the foot of the
hill on which the château was built. Here and there the

pergolas were roofed over by plants, then were open again to the sky, and for a time he found diversion in pacing off the gaps that were alternately in the shade and light. At some points the path widened into niches and recesses for a shrine in which various figures in sandstone stood: gods and goddesses which he had passed hundreds of times before without so much as giving them a thought or investigating what they represented. But today he stopped to look and was especially taken with those whose heads were missing, since they were the most mysterious and inscrutable ones and the ones whose identity was hardest to guess. At last, he walked all the way down the pergola and up it once more and down again and was now at the end of the village and heard it strike two. Or did the two strokes mark the half-hour, was it half-past two? No, it was only two.

He put an end to the continuous up and down of his walk and chose instead to proceed in a semicircle around the foot of the hill of the château until he was facing the château itself. Looking up at it, he saw the large terrace which, bordered by rows of potted orange trees and pyramidal cypresses, extended almost all the way down to the lake. It was separated from it only by a narrow strip of meadow, and in this particular meadow there stood an ancient oak around whose shade Schach walked in a circle, once, many times, as though tied to it by a spell. Plainly, the circle he was describing was reminding him of another one, for he kept murmuring: "If only I could break out of it!"

The water that came within such comparatively close range of the terrace of the château at this point was only a dead arm of the lake, not the lake itself. But going out on this lake in a boat had always been his greatest joy when he was a boy.

"If there's a boat I'll go out in it." And he walked up to the belt of rushes that lined the long inlet on three sides. There seemed to be no means of access anywhere. But finally he came upon an overgrown landing stage at the far end of which the large boat was moored that his mother had used for many years when rowing over to Karwe in the summer to visit the Knesebecks. There were oars and poles as well, while the boat's flat bottom was covered with a pile of rushes to keep things dry underfoot. Schach jumped in, unfastened the chain from the stake and pushed himself off. He had as yet no scope for any display of oarsmanship, the water being so shallow and narrow that he would have struck the rushes with each stroke of the oars. But presently the inlet broadened and he was now able to engage the oars. Everything was wrapped in deep silence, the day was not yet astir, and all that Schach perceived was a gentle rustling and soughing and the gurgling of the water lapping at the belt of rushes. At last he had come out into the great lake proper through which the Rhin flows, and the point that marked the undertow of the current could be clearly made out by a ruffle in the otherwise mirror-like smoothness of the surface. He guided the boat to move with the flow of the current, set it on the desired course, lay down on the pile of rushes, shipping the oars, and felt at once how the drifting and a gentle swaying were taking over.

The stars were becoming ever more faint, the sky was suffused in a reddish glow to the east, and he fell asleep.

When he woke up, the boat carried along by the current was already long past the point at which the dead arm of the lake branched off towards Wuthenow. He therefore took hold of the oars again and turned to with full force to get free of the current and to work his way back to the point he had overshot, relishing the exertion that this entailed.

Meanwhile day had broken. The sun stood suspended above the ridge of the manorial roof at Wuthenow, while on the shore opposite the clouds were aglow in the reflection and the contours of the wood were casting their shadow in the lake. But on the lake itself the first signs of life were beginning to stir, and a barge carrying peat, taking advantage of the early morning breeze, slid past Schach with outspread sail. He was seized with a shiver. But the shiver brought him relief, for he distinctly felt how the depression that had been weighing on him was subsiding. "Wasn't he taking it all too seriously? What did it amount to when all was said and done? Spite and ill will. And who can escape *that*? It's here today and gone tomorrow. Another week, and the malice will have run its course." But even as he was cheering himself up in this way, visions of other scenes loomed up as well, and he saw himself drawing up in a carriage on his rounds of the baronial estates to introduce Victoire von Carayon as his fiancée. And he distinctly overheard the old Princess,[2] Prince Ferdinand's wife, whispering to her daughter, the lovely Princess Radziwill: "*Est-elle riche?*" "*Sans doute.*" "Ah, *je comprends.*"[3]

Amid such shifting scenes and reflections he turned again into the cove that had been so peaceful shortly before, its rushes now throbbing with activity and life. The birds that had their nests there were screeching or cooing, some peewits were rising up in the air, and a wild duck, turning around with an inquisitive glance, dived under as the boat suddenly hove into view. Another minute, and Schach had pulled up at the landing stage again, wound the chain securely round the stake and, staying clear of any circuitous path, went up the terrace on whose topmost ledge he ran into Mother Kreepschen, already up to take the green fodder to her goat.

"Morning, Mother Kreepschen."

The old woman gave a start, seeing her young master, whom she had assumed to be indoors in the garden room (and for whose sake she had not let the hens out of the coop to avoid at all costs their cackling disturbing him in his sleep), coming toward her from the front part of the château.

"Why, young master. Wherever d'you come from?"

"I couldn't sleep, Mother Kreepschen."

"Anything happen then? Them ghosts on the loose again?"

"Almost. A visitation of moths and gnats. I'd left the candle burning. And one of the windows was open."

"But why didn't you blow out the lights? Everybody

knows where you've got light, you've always got moths and gnats. Did you ever! And me ole Kreepsch, he's gettin' more and more soft in the head too. My, my. And not a wink."

"I did sleep, Mother Kreepschen, in the boat, and quite well and soundly enough. But now I'm cold. And if there's a fire going you'll let me have something warm, won't you? Bit of soup or bit of coffee."

"Why, it's been on the fire all along, young master; fire's always the first thing. O' course, o' course, somethin' warm. And I'll bring it along in a minute, just that ole goat, it wants seein' to first. You've no idea, young master, what tricks such 'n ole goat'll get up to. She knows like she had a clock in her head whether it's five or six. And if it's six, she'll turn nasty. And if I try and milk her, well, what d'you suppose she'll do? Kick me, she will. And always smack in the small of me back, right near the hip. And why? 'cause she knows that's where I get me aches and pains. But now you'd better come on over to the parlor and sit down awhile. Me ole Kreepsch is with the horse, puttin' a little somethin' in for him to munch. But won't be more 'n quarter of 'n hour, young master, and you'll have your coffee. And somethin' to go with it. That ole baker's woman from Herzberg with the rolls been here already."

Following these remarks, Schach went into the Kreepschens' parlor. It all felt neat and clean inside except for the air. A strange odor pervaded the room caused by a mixture of pepper and coriander seeds that Mother Kreepschen had tucked into the corners of the sofa as a repellent against moths. Schach therefore opened the window, fastened the hook, and was only now able to take in with delight all the knickknacks with which the "parlor" was graced. Two small pictures from a calendar hung above the sofa, each illustrating an anecdote from the life of Frederick the Great. "Come, come," read the legend underneath one of them and that underneath the other: "*Bon soir, messieurs.*" The little pictures with their gold trimmings were framed by two heavy garlands of immortelles with black and white ribbons attached to them, while on the low, small stove stood a vase with quaking grass. But the ornament that took pride of place was a little red-roofed sentry box, in which a squirrel had most probably had its home at one time, complete with feeding trolley pulled along on a chain. Now there was no occupant and the trolley was standing idle.

Schach had just completed his inspection when he was informed that "over in his quarters everything was shipshape."

And true enough, when he entered the garden room that had so adamantly denied him shelter for the night, he was amazed at what tidiness and a devoted pair of hands had done with it since. Doors and windows were wide open, the room was flooded with the light of the morning sun, and all the dust had disappeared from the table and couch. Presently, Krist's wife duly appeared with the coffee, the rolls put into a basket, and just as Schach was about to take the lid off the little Meissen coffee pot, the sound of the church bells came drifting up from the village below.

"Whatever is *that*?" asked Schach. "It can hardly be seven yet."

"Just gone seven, young master."

"But it never used to start until eleven. And then the sermon at twelve."

"Yes, used to. But not any more. And always the third Sunday it's different. On two Sundays, when the one from Radensleben comes, it starts at twelve, 'cause he does his preachin' in Radensleben first, but on the third Sunday, when the ole man from Ruppin comes over, then it already begins at eight. And when ole Kriewitz here at his lookout in the belfry sees him takin' off over there, why, then he lets go with his bells. And that's always at seven."

"What's the name of the one who comes over now from Ruppin?"

"Why, what name would it be? It's what it always was. It's still ole Bienengräber."

"That's the one who confirmed me, you know. Was always a very decent man."

"Yes, that he is. Only, all his teeth are gone, not a single one left, and he mumbles and mutters so all the time nobody can make out a word."

"Can't be as bad as all that, Mother Kreepschen, surely. People, though, must always have something to grumble about. And of course, who more than the peasants! I think I'll go there, just to see once more what old Bienengräber can have to say to me, to me and the others. Has he still got that big horseshoe in his room that used to have a ten-pound weight dangling from it? I'd always keep my eyes glued to it when I found it too much to pay attention."

"Like as not he's still got it. Them boys never pay attention neither."

And with this she went off so as not to disturb her young master any longer, and promised to bring him a hymn book.

Schach had a hearty appetite and ate the Herzberg rolls with relish, having gone without a scrap of food since leaving Berlin. But at last he got up to stand in the garden door, and from here he took a look over the round bed and box-tree hedges and, beyond them, over the tree tops of the grounds until, at the foot of the hill, his eyes met a pair of storks ambling along a meadow streaked with red and yellow dock and ranunculus.

The contemplation of this scene evoked all kinds of thoughts, but the bells were ringing out a third time and so he went down into the village to listen from the manor choir stall "what old Bienengräber could have to say to him."

Bienengräber spoke effectively enough, truly from the heart and a knowledge of life, and when the last verse had been sung and the church was empty again Schach felt genuinely impelled to go into the vestry to express his appreciation to the old man for many an inspiring comment dating from the long-buried past and to escort him back in his boat across the lake. Then on their way over he would tell him everything, confess to him, and ask his advice. He would surely know the solution. Old age was always supposed to be wise, and if not owing to wisdom, at any rate because of the sheer fact of old age. "But," he checked himself even as he was formulating this plan, "what do I really want his solution for? Don't I know it in advance? Don't I find it in my inmost self? Don't I know the Commandments? What I lack is simply willingness to obey them."

And as he kept muttering to himself in this way he abandoned the idea of a talk and walked up the hill again to the château.

He had not been niggardly of this time in attending the service at church and yet, *even so*, it was only striking ten when he got back to the top of the hill.

Here he made the rounds of all the rooms, once, twice, looking at the portraits of all the Schachs hanging about singly or in clusters on the walls. All of them had occupied positions of high rank in the army, all of them were wearing the Black Eagle or the *pour le mérite*. *That* one was the general who had captured the big fortress near Malplaquet[4] and *this* one was the portrait of his own grandfather, the colonel in the Itzenplitz Regiment who had held the Hochkirch[5] churchyard for an hour with four hundred men. Eventually, he had fallen, cut up and shot to pieces, like all those who had been holding out with him. And hanging between them were the women, some of them beautiful, but the most beautiful of them all his mother.

When he had returned to the garden room, it was striking twelve. He flung himself into a corner of the sofa, covered his eyes and forehead with his hand, counting the strokes. "Twelve. I've now been here twelve hours, and it feels like twelve years . . . What will it be like? On weekdays the Krepschens and on Sundays Bienengräber or the one from Radensleben, which makes no difference. Birds of a feather. Decent folk, goes without saying, all a decent lot . . . And then I go rambling through the grounds with Victoire and on from the grounds to the meadow, the same meadow we look out on from the château day in and day out, forever and a day, and where dock and ranunculus are in bloom. And the storks picking their way through them. Perhaps there are just the two of us, or perhaps a little three-year-old is toddling alongside us, singing over and over: 'Storkie, I pray, bring a little sister my way.' And my ladyship is blushing and would like to have that little sister, *too*. And finally, eleven years are up, and we've covered the first stage, the first stage as far as what they call the 'staw-wreath wedding.' Strange word, that. And then, in due course, it'll be time for us to have our portraits painted, portraits for the gallery. For we certainly mustn't be missing! And I'll be taking up my position among all the generals as captain of the cavalry, and the beautiful ladies will be joined by Victoire. But I'll have a talk with the painter first, telling him: 'I count on your being able to bring out the *expression*. The soul makes for likeness.' Or shall I put it to him frankly: 'Do it gently . . .' No, no!"

XV

The Schachs and the Carayons

What always happens also happened in this instance: the Carayons had heard nothing of what was common knowledge practically all over town. On Tuesday, as usual, Aunt Marguerite appeared, thought Victoire "a little gaunt about the chin" and in the course of the conversation at the table remarked: "Well, haven't you heard, some caricatures are actually supposed to have been making the rounds." But this was as far as she went, since Aunt Marguerite belonged to those elderly ladies in society who always had only "been told" about all that was going on, and when Victoire asked: "Whatever are they about, dear aunt?" she merely replied: "Caricatures, my child. I know it absolutely for certain." And with this the subject was dropped.

It was surely fortunate for mother and daughter that they had failed to get wind of the sardonic and grotesque cartoons of which they were the object, but for the *third* party concerned, for Schach, it was just as surely unfortunate and a cause of new disagreements. If Frau von Carayon, whose finest sentiment could be said to be deep compassion, had only had the slightest inkling of all the wretchedness that had been visited upon her friend throughout this entire period, she would have, if not released him from the commitment exacted from him, at any rate granted him a reprieve and dispensed solace and sympathy. But lacking any knowledge of what had happened since, she became increasingly indignant at Schach and from the moment she learned of his withdrawal to Wuthenow, of his "breach of promise and faith," as she saw it, she delivered herself of the most scathing and unflattering pronouncements.

She learned of this withdrawal soon enough. On the very evening on which Schach had gone on leave, Alvensleben had himself announced at the Carayons'. Victoire, who felt ill at ease in the presence of all visitors, retired from the scene, but Frau von Caroyon asked that he be shown in and received him with conspicuous cordiality.

"I can't begin to tell you, dear Alvensleben, how delighted I am to see you again after all these weeks. There's been a world of developments since. And what a good thing that you stood your ground when they tried to foist Luther on you. That would have ruined your image for me for all time."

"And yet, madam, for a moment I was in two minds whether I ought to refuse."

"And why?"

"Because our mutual friend had declined immediately *before* me. I'm sick and tired of following in his footsteps time and again. As it is, there are quite enough people who make me out to be his second self, Zieten foremost among them, who called out to me only the other day: 'Take care, Alvensleben, that you don't find yourself listed in the billet and personnel roster as Schach II.' "

"Not much danger of that. After all, you're different."

"But no better."

"Who knows?"

"A question mark that comes as rather a surprise to me from the lips of my charming Frau von Carayon and which, if our pampered friend were to hear of it, might conceivably spoil his stay at Wuthenow."

"His stay at Wuthenow?"

"Yes, madam. On indefinite leave of absence. And you don't know about it? He can't have immured himself in his antique lakeside château, of which Nostitz the other day maintained that it was fifty percent worm-eaten and fifty percent romance, without saying goodbye to you?"

"And yet that's what happened. He's a man of moods, as you know."

She was tempted to enlarge on this but managed to restrain herself and to continue the conversation by touching on some of the day's news, from which Alvensleben was relieved to infer that she had not the remotest idea of the main topic of the day, the appearance of the cartoons. It had in fact never occurred to Frau von Carayon, even during the intervening several days, to try to find out anything more definite about what the aunt had alluded to.

Finally, Alvensleben took his leave, and Frau von Carayon, freed from all restraints, rushed in a flood of tears into Victoire's room to tell her of Schach's flight. For flight it was.

Victoire listened to every word. But, whether because of her confidence and faith or, on the contrary, her resignation, whichever it was, she remained calm.

"I beg you, don't jump to conclusions. There'll be a letter from him that will explain everything. Let's wait until then. You'll see that you've let yourself be swayed by your distrust and resentment of him more than was fair and proper."

But Frau von Carayon would not be persuaded to change her mind.

"I knew him even when you were still a child. Knew him only too well. He's vain and arrogant, and the baronial estates have completely turned his head. He's more and more laying himself open to ridicule. Believe me, he's out to achieve status and influence and is secretly harboring some sort of political or even governmental ambitions. What I resent more than anything is that he has suddenly remembered his Obodrite descent[1] and come to look on his Schach or Schach-clan heritage as something altogether extraordinary in the annals of world history."

"And so does no more than what *everybody* does . . . And the Schachs after all really *are* an old family."

"He's free to think it is and spread out his peacock's tail as he struts across his poultry yard. And poultry yards like that are a commonplace. But what good is that to *us*? Or at any rate to *you*? He could have afforded to stalk past me, snubbing the bourgeois farmer-general's daughter,[2] the little commoner. But you, Victoire, you; you aren't only my daughter, you're also your father's daughter, you are a *Carayon*!"

Victoire eyed her mother with a touch of mischievous surprise.

"Yes, go on, laugh, child, laugh loud and long, I wouldn't blame you. After all, you've seen me laugh about these things often enough myself. But Victoire, my sweet, the circumstances aren't the same, and today I ask your father's forgiveness and thank him from the bottom of my heart, since that aristocratic conceit of his, which used to drive me up the wall and in sheer boredom out of his presence, has armed me with a timely weapon to counter that to me insufferable snobbery. Schach, Schach! Who's Schach? I know nothing of their history and don't *want* to know anything about it. But I wager this brooch against a common pin that if you were to dump all their generations on the threshing floor where it's most exposed to the lash of the wind there'd be nothing left, I swear, but half a dozen colonels and captains of cavalry, all most piously dead and sporting a claret nose. You try and make me take up with people like *that*!"

"But Mama . . ."

"And as for the Carayons! True enough, their cradle didn't grace the banks of the Havel and not even of the Spree, and neither Brandenburg nor Havelberg Cathedral tolled its bells when one of their number arrived or

passed on. Oh, *ces pauvres gens, ces malheureux*[3] Carayons! They had their castles—*real* castles, by the way—
humbly enough along the banks of the Gironde,[4] were
humbly enough Girondists, and your father's own cous-
ins laid down their lives on the guillotine, because they
were both loyal and liberal and, undeterred by the
howls of the Mountain, had voted that the life of the
King be spared."

Victoire listened in ever greater amazement.

"However," Frau von Carayon went on, "I don't want
to talk about the latest events, about *today*. For I'm
perfectly aware that jogging along with one's age is always a crime in the eyes of those who were already on
the scene yesterday, never mind in what *garb*. No, I want
to talk about bygone days, the days when the first
Schach went to live in the country and on the shores of
Lake Ruppin and built a rampart and moat and listened
to mass in Latin without understanding a word. In those
very same days, the Carayons—*ces pauvres et malheureux* Carayons—joined in the march on Jerusalem,
conquering and liberating it. And when they'd returned
home, they were sought out by minstrels on their estates, and they were minstrels themselves. And when
Victoire de Carayon (yes, her name was also Victoire)
offered her hand to the eminent Count of Lusignan,
whose illustrious brother was a grand prior of the exalted order of Knights Hospitaller and eventually King
of Cyprus, we became the kith and kin by marriage of a
royal house, the Lusignans,[5] whose distinguished line
included the beautiful Melusine of unhappy but, thank
God, unprosaic memory. And us Carayons, whose vista

has taken in very different horizons, this Schach man proposes to turn his back on and contemptuously give the slip? *Us* he professes to be ashamed of? He, Schach. Is he trying to do this as Schach or as squire of Wuthenow? Oh, bah! What do they both add up to? Schach is a blue tunic with a red collar and Wuthenow is a mud hut."

"Mama, believe me, you're being unfair to him. I try to view it in a different perspective. And that's where I see it too."

Frau von Carayon bent down to Victoire and kissed her with deep emotion.

"Oh, how good you are, ever so much better than your mama. And there's only one thing to be said for her: that she loves you. But he ought to love you, too, if only for your humility."

Victoire smiled.

"No, not in that way. The notion that you're a pauper and an outcast has come to obsess you with the persistence of a fixed idea. You *aren't* such a pauper. And he too . . ."

She hesitated.

"Look here. You were a lovely child, and Alvensleben was telling me in what enthusiastic terms the Prince only the other day had spoken again of how lovely you looked at the Massov ball. That isn't gone, that's still part of you, and anyone disposed in heart and mind to look for it in your features with affection is bound to see it. And if anyone ought to, it's *he*! But he refuses to, for he's as conventional as he's arrogant. A timid little conformist. He listens to what people say, and when a man behaves like that (*we* have no choice), I call it cowardice and lack of moral fiber. But I'll bring him to book. I've laid my plans and am going to make him eat humble pie as surely as he has tried to make *us* eat it."

Following this conversation, Frau von Carayon returned to the corner room and, sitting down at Victoire's small writing table, wrote:

Herr von Alvensleben has given me to understand that you, Herr von Schach, have today, Saturday evening, left Berlin and have decided on a stay in the country at Wuthenow. I have no reason to begrudge you this stay in the country or dispute your right to it. However, against your legitimate right I must weigh that of my daughter. And so you will allow me to remind you that we had agreed that the announcement of the engagement was to be made tomorrow, Sunday. I continue to insist on this announcement no less today. If it has not taken place by Wednesday morning, I shall resort to other steps, entirely at my discretion. Contrary as this would be to my nature (not to mention Victoire's, who knows nothing of this letter and would only try to stop me), the circumstances which, to say the least, you know only too well leave me no alternative. Until Wednesday then.

Josephine von Carayon

She sealed the letter and handed it personally to a messenger with instructions to set out for Wuthenow at daybreak.

He had expressly been told not to wait for an answer.

XVI

Frau von Carayon
and Old General Köckritz

Wednesday came and went without a letter from
Schach, let alone the announcement of the engagement
that was to have been made. Frau von Carayon had
expected as much and provided for it accordingly.

Thursday morning a carriage drew up in front of the
house which was to take her to Potsdam, where the King
had been in residence for some weeks. She intended to
go down on her knees, to give him an account of the
affront to which she had been subjected, and to appeal
to him for help. That it would be within the King's
power to extend to her such help and to set matters right
seemed to her beyond question. She had also thought
about the ways and means of gaining access to His Majesty, and to good effect. She knew the Adjutant General
von Köckritz, who more than thirty years before as a

young lieutenant or captain on the general staff had been a frequent visitor in her parents' house and brought "little Josephine," the spoiled child, many a box of sweets. He was now the favorite of the King, the most influential person of his immediate entourage, and she was hoping that through *him*, with whom she had at least kept up formal relations, she could consider herself assured of an audience.

Toward noon, Frau von Carayon arrived on the other side of the river. She put up at the "Hermit," changed, and immediately set out for the palace. Here, however, she was confronted with the news by a chamberlain, who happened to be coming down the front steps at that moment, that His Majesty had since left Potsdam again and gone to meet Her Majesty the Queen. Her Majesty was expected back from Pyrmont next day at Paretz where, free from the constraints of life at court, they were hoping to spend a week in peaceful seclusion.

This was bad news indeed. He who is embarking on a disagreeable errand (even if it entailed the disagreeably dire straits of the gallows) and is longing for the grim finale finds nothing more intolerable than a delay. Make haste, make haste! One can hold on for a brief spell, but then one's nerve gives way.

Dismayed and troubled by the thought that this piece of bad luck might betoken bad luck altogether, Frau von Carayon returned to the inn. To contemplate driving on to Paretz today was out of the question, all the more so as one could not possibly request an audience so late in the afternoon. Nothing for it then but to wait until tomorrow! She had a modest meal, at any rate sat down at table, and seemed determined to pass the long, interminable hours of solitude in her room. But the thoughts and visions taking shape in her mind and above all the solemn speech she kept repeating to herself for the hundredth time, kept on repeating to herself until she finally felt she would not be able to utter a word at the psychological moment—all this gave her the sound idea, come what may, to shake free of these ruminations and to go for a drive through the streets and environs of the town. A hired footman duly appeared to offer her his services, and at six o'clock a hackney carriage in reasonably presentable state pulled up in front of the inn, as the conveyance from Berlin, after contending for half a day with the sandy soil in the summer heat, had turned out to be definitely in need of a rest.

"Where may I take your ladyship?"

"I leave it to you. No castles, though, or at least no more than you can help. But any parks and gardens and water and meadows."

"Ah, *je comprends*," the footman fumbled in French, having come to take it for granted that his visitors from out of town were invariably half-French, or also perhaps feeling he ought to register some awareness of Frau von Carayon's French name. And he ordered the coachman in his braided hat on the box to drive first of all to the New Gardens.

In the New Gardens everything seemed desolate, and a dark, lugubrious avenue of cypresses stretched on and on apparently without end. Finally, they turned into a

lane bordered by a single row of trees alongside a lake,
its surface played on by the sprawling, drooping
branches. But the trelliswork of the foliage was spar-
kling in the gleam and glitter of the setting sun. The
beauty of the scene made Frau von Carayon forget all
her troubles, and she only felt its spell broken when the
carriage turned off the lakeside drive back into the
broad avenue and presently pulled up in front of a man-
sion built of brick, but lavishly adorned with inlaid gold
and marble.

"Whom does it belong to?"

"To the King."

"And what is it called?"

"The Marble Palace."

"Ah, the Marble Palace. So this is the palace . . ."

"At your service, madam. This is the palace in which
His Majesty King Frederick William II[1] was called to his
Maker after his long and painful bout of dropsy. And
inside everything's been left just as it was then. I know
the room like the palm of my hand where His Majesty,
bless his soul, was always given the 'gas of life' by Councilor Hufeland[2] in a little balloon or calf's bladder was
maybe all it was. Would your ladyship like to take a
look at the room? Of course, it's late, but I know the
valet, and I'm sure he'll show you around if I put in a
word . . . goes without saying . . . And happens to be the
same small room in which there's a sculpture of Frau
Rietz[3] or, as some call her, Demoiselle Encken or
Countess Lichtenau, only a small sculpture, I mean just
down to the hips, or not even."

Frau von Carayon declined with thanks. In anticipation of her errand the following day she was in no mood to explore the inner sanctum of Frau Rietz or even only her bust. She therefore expressed a wish to keep on driving further into the interior of the park and only gave directions for turning back when the sun was already low and a cooler breeze was heralding the onset of evening. It was in fact striking nine as they passed the garrison church on their return and before the chimes had finished their carillon, the carriage had drawn up at the "Hermit" again.

The drive had proved bracing and restored her fortitude. A soothing fatigue also did its share and she slept better than she had for a long time. Even her dreams were bright and cheerful.

The following morning, her Berlin carriage, now fully recovered, appeared in front of the hotel as arranged. However, as she had every reason to be wary of her own coachman's knowledge of the area and judgment, she engaged, as an extra, as it were, the same footman who, for all the little eccentricities of his trade, had on the previous day shown himself so perfectly reliable. He acquitted himself equally well today. He was informative about every village and manorial retreat they passed, especially about Marquardt, where a little summer residence gleaming across the park aroused briefly at least Frau von Carayon's curiosity. It was there that, aided and abetted by General von Bischofswerder,[4] the "fat King" (as the cicerone in increasingly familiar tone bluntly put it) had seen ghosts.

A quarter of a mile beyond Marquardt, they had to cross the Wublitz, a tributary of the Havel covered with water lilies in bloom, then they passed farmland and meadows in which grass and flowers had grown to a great height. And it was not yet noon when they came to a footbridge and presently to an open iron gate, which marked the entrance to the park of Paretz.

Frau von Carayon, fully aware of her role as a supplicant and prompted by a characteristic delicacy, stopped the carriage at this point and got out, to cover the rest of the way on foot. From here it was only a short walk in the sun, but it was precisely the sun that bothered her and she kept close to the side of the road under the trees lest she be seen too soon.

At last she reached the sandstone steps of the château and bravely walked up. The imminence of the danger had partly restored her usual resolution.

"I wish to speak to General von Köckritz," she addressed a footman in the vestibule, whom the entrance of the elegant lady had immediately brought to his feet.

"Whom have I the honor to announce to the General?"

"Frau von Carayon."

The footman bowed and brought back word that the General desired her ladyship to be shown into the anteroom.

Frau von Carayon did not have long to wait. General von Köckritz, of whom it was said that his only passion besides his ardent love for his King was a pipeful of tobacco and a rubber at whist, came toward her from his study, at once recalled the old days and invited her with a most courtly gesture to be seated. His whole bearing betrayed so clearly a person of kindness and one who inspired trust that the question of his intelligence meant very little by comparison, especially for those who, like Frau von Carayon, had come with a request. And at court they are the majority. He fully bore out the theory that a *kindly* entourage of a prince is always greatly to be preferred to a brilliant one. Except, of course, that these private servants of a prince must not aspire to public service as well nor to a voice in the decisions and conduct of government.

General von Köckritz had so seated himself that Frau von Carayon saw him in profile. The lower half of his head was imprisoned in the enormously high, stiff collar of his uniform, with a jabot billowing out in front, while a short, neatly fashioned pigtail was hanging down at the back. It seemed to lead a life of its own, swinging gently to and fro with a touch of coquetry, even when the man himself did not show the slightest movement.

Frau von Carayon, without forgetting the gravity of her situation, was obviously amused at this curiously playful diversion, and now that her spirits were raised, the task before her seemed a good deal easier and simpler to manage, so that she felt able to talk freely about a wide variety of matters, including *that* subject which might be called the "delicate point" of the problem with which she, or her daughter, was faced.

The General listened with a sympathetic as well as an attentive ear, and when Frau von Carayon had finished, he said:

"Yes, madam, these are very unfortunate things, things such as His Majesty is not pleased to hear, so that I usually keep them to myself, always assuming of course that there is no possible remedy and that nothing whatever is to be done to help. But here something *is* to be done to help, and I should be remiss in my duty and render His Majesty poor service if I were to withhold a case like yours from him or, since you have come to present it in person, madam, if I tried to put deliberately contrived difficulties in your way. For such difficulties are invariably contrived in a country like ours, where from time immemorial princes and kings have had the rights of their people at heart and not expediently sought to evade the implementation of those rights. Least of all my gracious King and Master, who is profoundly sensitive to the *fairness* of these rights, and for this very reason has a genuine dislike of and outright antipathy to all *those* who, like certain gentlemen of the officer corps, notably the otherwise honorable and valiant officers of the said Gensdarmes Regiment, are prone through misguided conceit to indulge in all sorts of mischief, thinking it is perfectly proper and commendable, certainly not at all wrong, to sacrifice the happiness and reputation of others on the altar of their reckless *moralité*."

Frau von Carayon's eyes filled with tears.

"Que vous êtes bon, mon cher Général."[5]

"Not I, madam, it's my gracious King and Master who is the kind one. And I believe you will shortly have tangible proof of his kindheartedness, despite the fact that this is a bad—or shall we say difficult—day for us today. For, as you may already have heard, the King is expecting the Queen back in a few hours, and it's to ensure that nothing would intrude upon their joyful re-union that he is here, *that*'s what has made him come to Paretz. And now he is being pursued to this idyllic place with a legal matter, a controversy, and one of such a delicate nature at that. Yes, Fortuna has certainly cut a caper there and played him a freakish trick. Here he is, looking forward to the felicities of love (you know how great a love he bears the Queen), and almost at the very moment that is to see his happiness come true, he hears a story of unhappy love. That puts him into a bad humor. But he is too generous not to rise above such bad humor, and if we even remotely succeed in striking the right note we should also be able to reap from the very concurrence of the circumstances a distinct gain. For the prospect of his own happiness will have the effect of making him all the more inclined to dispel the clouds that darken the happiness of others. I know him thor-oughly where his sense of justice and kindness of heart are concerned. And now, madam, I propose to announce your visit to the King."

But suddenly he hesitated as if debating with himself and, turning around again, added:

"If I'm not mistaken, he's just gone out into the gar-dens of the château. I know his favorite spot. So let me see what I can do. I shall be back in a few minutes and let you know whether he will receive you or not. And once again: take heart. There's hope."

With these words he reached for his hat and stick and went out by a small side door that opened on to the grounds of the château.

The walls of the reception room where Frau von Carayon had stayed were hung with an assortment of color prints of the kind fashionable in England at the time: heads of angels by Sir Joshua Reynolds, landscapes by Gainsborough, also several reproductions of Italian masterpieces, among them a penitent Mary Magdalene. Was it the one by Correggio?[6] The robe in marvelous dark blue shades, which almost completely shrouded the figure of the repentant woman, captured Frau von Carayon's attention. She went up close to verify the painter's name, but before she could make it out the General had come back and asked his protégée to follow him.

And thereupon they went into the park of the château where everything was silent and still. The path, winding in and out between birch trees and silver firs, led to an artificial wall of rock overgrown with ivy. The King was seated on a stone bench in front of it (old Köckritz having remained behind).

When he saw the elegant lady approaching, he got up and went toward her with a sedate and affable air. Frau von Carayon made as if to curtsy, but the King would not allow it and took hold of her hand as though to help her up, saying:

"Frau von Carayon? Remember very well indeed . . . Recall children's ball . . . lovely daughter . . . at that time . . ."

He paused for a moment, either out of embarrassment at this last remark he had let slip or because he was touched by the sight of the unhappy mother almost trembling with emotion as she stood before him, and continued:

"Köckritz just been dropping hints . . . *Very* unfortunate . . . But please . . . be seated, madam . . . Courage . . . And now tell me."

XVII

Schach in Charlottenburg

A week later the King and Queen had left Paretz, and the very next day Captain of the Cavalry von Schach, complying with a royal summons served on him at Château Wuthenow, was making his way on horseback to Charlottenburg, where the Court had since removed. He took the road through Brandenburg Gate and along the great Tiergarten boulevard, closely followed on his left by his orderly Baarsch, a redhead full of freckles like a dish of lentils and with whiskers redder still. About which reddish hue and somewhat bristling beard Zieten was wont to maintain that this specimen of a perch, too, could be recognized by his fins.* A native son of Wuthenow and former playmate of his captain and lord of the manor, he was of course loyalty itself in his devotion to him and to everything bearing the name of Schach.

* Wordplay on *Barsch* (perch).

It was four o'clock in the afternoon and there was not much traffic, even though the sun was shining and a refreshing breeze was blowing. They only met a handful of riders, including some officers from Schach's regiment. Schach returned their salute, passed the Landwehrgraben and presently turned into the broad Charlottenburg avenue with its summer houses and front gardens.

At the Turkish Pavilion,[1] which was in fact normally his destination, his horse wanted to turn in that direction, but he reined it in and did not stop until he had come to Café Morello, which today was a location more convenient to him for the errand on which he was bound. He leaped from the saddle, handed the reins to his orderly and went straight off to the Palace. There, after crossing a derelict quadrangle covered with grass long since scorched by the July sun, he entered first a spacious entrance hall and presently a narrow corridor on whose walls there were drawn up, in obviously larger than life-size portraits, the goggle-eyed blue giants of Frederick the Great. But at the end of this passage he came upon a footman who, after first announcing his arrival, conducted him to the King's study.

The King was standing at a desk spread with maps, some situation maps of the battle of Austerlitz. He immediately turned around, went toward Schach, saying:

"Have sent for you, dear Schach . . . Frau von Carayon . . . unfortunate business; don't like acting the moralist and petty faultfinder; hate it; my own share of blunders. But mustn't stay bogged down in blunders; make amends. By the way, don't quite understand. Handsome woman, the mother; liked her *very* much; intelligent woman."

Schach bowed.

"And the daughter! Know about it of course, know it, poor child . . . All the same, must have found her attractive. And what one has once found attractive one must surely, with a little effort, find so again. But that's *your* affair, doesn't concern me. What does concern me is *honnêteté*. And for the sake of this *honnêteté* I insist on your marriage to Fräulein von Carayon. Unless you should be prepared to resign and leave the service."

Schach made no reply, but implied by his demeanor and expression that this would be to him the most grievous blow of all.

"Well, then, staying on; good man; like that. But reparation must be made, and quickly, and at once. By the way, old family, the Carayons, and won't hurt the prospects of your daughters (beg pardon, dear Schach) for admission to the noblewomen's home of Marienfliess or Heiligengrabe.² It's agreed then. Count on it, insist on it. And are going to send me word."

"At your service, Your Majesty."

"And one more thing; have spoken about it to the Queen; wants to see you; woman's notion. Are going to find her on the other side in the orangery . . . Thank you."

Schach was graciously dismissed, he bowed and walked down the corridor toward the big glass-covered greenhouse of which the King had spoken in the opposite wing of the Palace.

But the Queen was not yet there, was perhaps still in the grounds. He therefore went outside again, pacing up and down on the flagstone path among an array of Roman emperors that had been put up here, some of whom seemed to be eyeing him with a faunlike leer. At last he saw the Queen coming toward him from the direction of the ferryboat landing stage, attended by a lady-in-waiting, the younger Fräulein von Viereck, it seemed. He went to meet the two ladies and at the appropriate distance stood aside to render the prescribed salute. The lady-in-waiting, for her part, kept a few paces behind.

"I am glad to see you, Herr von Schach. You are coming from the King."

"At your service, Your Majesty."

"It's a little irregular that I have asked that you come to see me. But the King, who was originally opposed to it and teased me about it, eventually consented. It's just that I'm a woman and it would be harsh if I had to renounce my woman's way just because I happen to be a *Queen*. As a woman I am interested in everything that concerns our sex, and what could be of greater concern to us than such a *question d'amour*."

"Your Majesty is most gracious."

"Not toward you, dear Schach. It's for the young lady's sake . . . The King has told me everything and Köckritz has added his share. I learned of it on the very day I got back to Paretz from Pyrmont, and I can't begin to tell you how greatly my sympathy for the young lady was aroused. And now you, *you* of all people, want to deny the dear child this feeling of sympathy and together with this feeling of sympathy her rights. That's inconceivable. I have known you for such a long time and always found you to be a gentleman and a man of integrity. And I think we had better leave it at that. I have heard about the caricatures that have been circulating and these cartoons, or so I imagine, have unnerved you and got the better of your considered judgment. I can understand that, knowing only too well from bitter personal experience how wounding such things are and how the poisonous arrow not only lacerates our feelings but also works a change in us, and not for the better. But however that may be, it behooved you to take stock of yourself and at the same time of *that* which duty and honor demand of you."

Schach made no reply.

"And you *will* do so," the Queen continued, growing increasingly more animated, "and prove yourself repentant and contrite. It can't be difficult for you, since even the accusation against you, so the King assured me, had still contained an undertone of affection. Do remember this should your resolution ever again be in danger of weakening, which I can't think it will. Certainly, there's little that would so please me just now as the settling of this dispute and the union of two hearts that seem to me to be meant for each other. Out of a really true love too. For you won't deny, I trust, that it was a mysterious quality that drew you to this dear and once so lovely child. I could not bring myself to believe that the contrary was true. And now quickly go home and spread happiness and be happy yourself! You have my every good wish, *both* of you. You will keep in the background for as long as circumstances require, but in any event I expect you to send me news of your family affairs and to have the name of your Queen entered as the first godmother in your parish register at Wuthenow. And now Godspeed."

A parting nod and friendly wave of the hand accompanied these words, and Schach, turning around once more near the gate of the park, saw the two ladies passing into a side path and marking for a shadier part of the park nearer the Spree.

He himself was on his mount again a quarter of an hour later; his orderly Baarsch followed behind.

The gracious remarks of both their Majesties had not failed to make an impression on him; nevertheless, he had only been shaken, but in no sense had undergone a change of heart. He knew what he owed the King: *obedience*! But his heart rebelled, and he therefore had to devise a scheme that would combine obedience and disobedience in one, would in equal measure accord with the command of his King and the dictates of his own nature. And this left only *one* way. An idea he had already conceived at Wuthenow now occurred to him again and quickly ripened into a resolve, and the more firmly he felt it taking shape, the more he regained his earlier composure and calm. "Living," he muttered to himself. "What's living? A question of minutes, a change from today to tomorrow." And for the first time after days of intense strain he felt at ease and free once more.

When, on his ride home, he had got to the point in the road where an avenue of old chestnut trees branched off in the direction of Kurfürstendamm, he turned into this avenue and, motioning Baarsch over to him, said as he dropped the reins and with his left hand rested on the horse's croup:

"Tell me, Baarsch, what do you really think of marriage?"

"Why, captain, sir, what am I supposed to think of it? My father, God rest his soul, always used to say: to marry is a good thing, but not to marry is better still."

"Yes, he may well have said that. But now, suppose *I* were to get married, Baarsch?"

"Why, captain, sir, you're not seriously going to!"

"Yes, who knows . . . Would it really be such a disaster?"

"Why, captain, sir, not for *you* so much, but for me . . ."

"How so?"

"Because I've made a bet with Corpor'l Czepanski that nothing would come of it *after all*. And the loser's got to stand all the corpor'ls a drink."

"But how did you all know about it?"

"Oh, gosh, there's been rumors all along. And then when the cartoons turned up too last week . . ."

"Oh, I see . . . Well, now, Baarsch, how much did you really bet? A lot?"

"Hm, well, so-so, captain, sir. A Cottbus beer and kümmel. But for the whole gang."

"Well, Baarsch, we won't let you be out of pocket because of that. I'll pay the bet."

And then he fell silent, just muttering to himself: ". . . *et payer les pots cassés.*"[3]

XVIII

Fata Morgana[1]

Schach got home again in good time and that same evening wrote a letter to Frau von Carayon in which, in ostensibly sincere words, he offered his apology for his conduct. A royal summons he had received at Wuthenow the day before yesterday had taken him over to Charlottenburg this afternoon where the King and Queen had reminded him of *that* which constituted his duty. He regretted having been in need of such a reminder, considered the step Frau von Carayon had taken justified, and asked to be allowed to call on the two ladies in the course of the following morning in order to repeat to them in person his regret at these renewed sins of omission. A postscript longer than the letter itself added that he had passed through a crisis, but that he had now got over this crisis and felt he could safely say that there would *not* again be any grounds for doubts about him or his sense of justice. His life was now exclusively given

over to the one desire and concern to make up for all
that had happened through legitimation. On anything
over and beyond this he was for the time being commit-
ting himself to silence.

This letter, which was delivered by the little groom,
was, despite the late hour, answered by Frau von
Carayon then and there. She was pleased to note that he
had written in such conciliatory terms. Everything that
according to his letter was to be regarded as belonging
to the past had best be passed over in silence; *she*, too,
felt she ought to have proceeded with more patience
and discretion, she had let her feelings run away with
her, and only the *one* factor that might be allowed to
exonerate her was that she had not learned of those malicious attacks in drawing and print which seemed to
have given rise to his conduct during the previous week
until two days ago. Had she known about this before she
would have taken a more lenient view of many things, at
any rate adopted toward him and his silence a more
forbearing attitude. Her hope now was that everything
would again be in harmonious accord. Victoire's great
love (all too great) and his own attitude, which, she felt
convinced, while it might fluctuate, could not be per-
manently shaken, gave her every assurance of a peaceful
and, if her pleas met with response, also of a happy
future.

The following morning Schach was announced at
Frau von Carayon's. She went up to him and the conversation that immediately ensued betrayed less embarrassment on either side than one would have expected after

all that had happened. And yet one could also account for it. Everything that had happened, however painful in its effect at either end, had none the less met with understanding by both parties, and where there is understanding there is forgiveness as well, or at any rate the possibility of it. Everything had come about as the natural outcome of the circumstances, and neither the escape Schach had resorted to nor the complaint Frau von Carayon had made in the highest quarters had meant to imply malevolence or spite.

When the conversation was momentarily about to flag, Victoire came in. She was looking very well, not drawn, if anything more animated than usual. He went toward her, not in a cold and stiffly formal, but in a warm and outgoing manner, and the expression of a sincere and deeply felt sympathy with which he looked at her and held out his hand to her set the seal upon the reconciliation. There was no doubt about it, he was moved, and while Victoire was radiant with joy her mother's eyes filled with tears.

This was her chance for striking the iron. She therefore asked Schach, who had already got up, to be so good as to sit down again for a moment or two so that between them they could work out the most urgent arrangements. What she had to say was only a few words. One thing was certain, time had been lost, and no doubt the first thing to do was to make up for this loss. Her many long years of friendship with consistorial councilor Bocquet, who had officiated at her own marriage and confirmed Victoire, provided the best means for

doing so. It should be easy to substitute a single posting
of the banns for the traditional three times; that would
have to be done on Sunday next, and on Friday of the
week thereafter—for Fridays, generally regarded as
days of bad luck, had in her experience proved quite the
reverse—this would have to be followed by the wedding. And of course in her house, as she had an absolute
horror of weddings at a hotel or an inn. As for subse-
quent plans, that was up to the young couple; she
was wondering whether Venice would win out over
Wuthenow or Wuthenow over Venice. The lagoons
were a common feature of both, and so was the gondola,
and there was just one thing she would ask: that the
little footbridge below the rushes where the gondola
was moored would never be elevated to the Bridge of
Sighs.[2]

This was how the conversation and the visit went.

Sunday, as arranged, saw the posting of the banns and
the Friday on which the wedding was to take place was
approaching. Everybody in the Carayon household was
in a state of excitement, the most excited of all Aunt
Marguerite, who was coming every day and by her in-
genuous enthusiasm made up for all the irritations that
were normally part and parcel of her presence.

In the evening Schach called. He was more cheerful
and more considerate in his comments than was his
wont and only avoided, as noticeably as it luckily went
unnoticed, any mention of the wedding and the prepara-
tions for it. When asked whether he wished things to be
done in this way or that, he earnestly entreated them to

feel free to proceed entirely as they saw fit; he knew the ladies' tact and good taste and was satisfied that everything would be decided for the best without any advice or contribution from him; if, as a result, he was left in the dark and mystified by a number of things this would, if anything, be rather an advantage for him, having from childhood had a fondness for being taken by surprise.

By such subterfuges he evaded all talk that, as Aunt Marguerite put it, "had *en vue* the great day," but grew all the more voluble when the conversation touched on their travel plans *after* the wedding. For Venice, in spite of Frau von Carayon's veiled objections, had after all carried the day against Wuthenow, and Schach, whenever the subject came up, dilated with what were for him altogether unwonted leaps of the imagination on every conceivable itinerary and foreign scene. He proposed to cross over to Sicily and sail past the islands of the Sirens,[3] "whether unfettered or tied to the mast he would leave to Victoire and her trust." And then they would want to go on to Malta. Not because of Malta, oh, certainly not. But on the way to it there would be the site where the mysterious Dark Continent would for the very first time hold discourse in reflections and mirages with the Hyperborean native of fog and snow. *That* was the site where the resplendent fairy dwelt, the *mute* Siren, who by the magic of her colors almost exceeded in seductive allure the singing one. The figures and scenes projected by her magic lantern would be constantly shifting: a weary column trekking across the yellow sand might suddenly give way to a widening expanse of green meadowland, and seated under a shading palm would be a cluster of men, heads lowered and every pipe aglow, and black- and brown-skinned girls, their braids undone and skirts tucked up as for a dance, would be raising their cymbals and beating their tambourines. And now and then there would be a sound that suggested laughter. And then all would fall silent and vanish again. And this mirage in the mysterious distance, *that* was the goal!

And Victoire exclaimed with joy, carried away by the fervor of his description.

Yet at the same time she was seized by a sense of dread and gloom, and in the depths of her soul a voice was calling: *Fata Morgana.*

XIX

The Wedding

The marriage ceremony had been performed, and at four o'clock the guests invited to the wedding were assembling in the large dining room which, looking out on the courtyard, was normally thought of as a merely awkward appendage of the Carayons' flat and was being used again today for the first time for a good many years. This seemed expedient, even though the number of guests was not large. Old consistorial councilor Bocquet had allowed himself to be persuaded to come to the feast and was seated, facing the bridal pair, beside Frau von Carayon. Among the other guests, apart from Aunt Marguerite and some old friends from the days of the farmers-general,[1] mention must be made above all of Nostitz, Alvensleben, and Sander. Schach, for all his apathy that had been noticed even in the compiling of the list of prospective guests, had laid particular stress on the latter's presence, having meanwhile learned of the tact he had shown on the occasion of the proposed circulation of the three cartoons, a conduct Schach appreciated all the more for not having expected it from *that* quarter. Bülow, Schach's old adversary, was no longer in Berlin and would presumably have been absent even if he had still been there.

The mood at table until the first toast was proposed continued in the tone of traditional solemnity. But the signal for a change of mood was given when the old consistorial councilor had spoken and finished with what might be called a toast in "historical retrospect" under three headings, invoking, first, the grandfather's manor from the period of the farmers-general, then Frau von Carayon's wedding, thirdly Victoire's confirmation (including the quotation of the text from the Bible with which she had been speeded on her pilgrimage), and, finally, a half-reverent, half-jocular reference to the "sacred bird of Egypt,[2] whose auspicious clime was marked out for a visit." They all surrendered to an atmosphere of free and easy gaiety with which even Victoire fell in, and not least when the aunt, wearing a dress of leafgreen silk and a large tortoiseshell comb in honor of the occasion, rose to propose a *second* toast to the bride and bridegroom. Her bashful tapping of the decanter of water with the fruit knife had for some time gone unnoticed and was only heeded when Frau von Carayon announced Aunt Marguerite would like to speak.

She duly bowed by way of corroboration and launched into her speech with much more self-assurance

than one would have expected from her initial diffidence.

"The consistorial councilor has spoken so movingly
and at such length and I am merely the woman Ruth
who went to the field to glean among the ears of corn,
which was also the passage that was the subject of the
sermon last Sunday in the little melon-steeple church,
which was quite empty again, I believe only eleven or
twelve people. But as the aunt of the dear bride, in
which capacity I am probably the oldest, I raise my
glass to drink once more to the young couple's health."

And then she sat down again to receive everybody's
compliments. Schach tried to kiss the old lady's hand,
which she would not permit, whereas she responded to
Victoire's embrace with sundry little demonstrations of
affection, assuring her at the same time she had known it
all from the start, ever since they had taken the drive to
Tempelhof and the walk to the church. For she had
certainly seen that Victoire besides the large bunch of
violets intended for her mama had also been holding a
small one in her hand which she had meant to give to
the dear bridegroom, Herr von Schach, at the door of
the church. But when he had got there, she had thrown
the small bunch away and it had landed close by the
door on top of a child's grave, which was always significant and equally so on *this* occasion. For however much
opposed to superstition she was, she did believe in
mutual attraction, when the moon was on the wane of
course. And the entire afternoon was still as vividly present in her mind as though it had been yesterday, and if

some people pretended to be blind, one did after all have a perfectly good pair of eyes in one's head and was able to tell well enough where the best cherries were to be found. She became more and more enamored of this phrase without any more light being shed for all that on its meaning.

Following Aunt Marguerite's toast, they all changed seats, everybody abandoning his in an attempt to hold the center of the stage in turn now here, now there. Presently the big epigram-filled pieces of pastry from Café Josty were passed around and, despite the small and illegible scrawls, such messages as "Dear, adorable elf, even your woe inflicts no woe" were deciphered and read out. Then they all rose from the table. Alvensleben escorted Frau von Carayon, Sander, Aunt Marguerite, which inspired Sander to some good-natured badinage in allusion to the subject of Ruth, badinage that so delighted the aunt that she whispered to Victoire as the coffee was being served:

"Charming gentleman. And so polite. And so profound."

Schach was talking at great length to Sander; he inquired after Bülow, with whom he had admittedly never found himself in tune, but who, for all his fixed ideas, had always interested him, and he asked Sander to convey this to him when he had an opportunity. All that he said bespoke friendliness and a desire for reconciliation.

He was not the only one, though, in this desire for reconciliation, but was joined in it by Frau von Carayon. As she was personally handing him his second cup, while he was helping himself to the sugar bowl, she said:

"A word with you, dear Schach, but in the next room." And she led the way.

"Dear Schach," she began, sitting down on a sofa with a large floral pattern from where they both, the folding door being open, had an unobstructed view of the corner room, "these are our last few moments together and I should like, before we say goodbye, to unburden myself of a number of things. I don't want to be coy about my age, but a year is a long time, and who knows whether we shall see each other again. No need for any words about Victoire. She won't cause you a dark hour: she loves you too much to be capable of it or to want to. And you, dear Schach, will prove yourself worthy of her love. You won't hurt her, the lovely creature, who is all humility and devotion. You couldn't possibly. And so I won't extract a promise from you. I know I have it in advance."

Schach was looking in front of him as Frau von Carayon delivered herself of these remarks and, holding the cup in his left hand, he let the coffee drip in a slow trickle from the delicately wrought little spoon.

"Since our reconciliation," she continued, "I have regained my trust. But this ability to trust, as already pointed out in my letter to you, had deserted me, during the days that now fortunately belong to the past, to a far greater extent than I would have thought possible, and in those days I had harsh words for you when speaking to Victoire, and harsher ones still when I was by myself.

I accused you of being mean and arrogant, vain and spineless, and, worst of all, taxed you with ingratitude and deception. And now I repent and am ashamed of a mood that could make me so unmindful of the old days."

She paused for a moment. But when Schach wanted to reply she would not let him, saying:

"Just one more thing. Everything I said and thought in those days has been weighing on me and has made me long for this confession. It's only now that everything between us is open and aboveboard again and that I can look you straight in the eye again. But enough of this. Come, let us go. They will have been looking for us as it is."

And taking his arm, she quipped:

"Isn't it so: *on revient toujours à ses premiers amours?*[3] And what a good thing I can say this to you laughingly and in a moment of pure and unqualified joy."

Victoire went up to her mother from the direction of the corner room, saying:

"Well, what was it?"

"A declaration of love."

"I thought so. And a good thing, Schach, that we're setting out tomorrow. Isn't it? I wouldn't for the life of me like to present the image of a jealous daughter to the world."

And mother and daughter sat down on the sofa where they were joined by Alvensleben and Nostitz.

At that very moment Schach was told that his carriage had arrived and it seemed as though on being given this information he changed color. Frau von

Carayon noticed it as well. But he quickly collected himself again, took his leave, and went out into the hallway where the little groom was waiting for him with hat and coat. Victoire followed him to the staircase, which was caught in a last glimmer of daylight from the courtyard.

"Until tomorrow," Schach said, hurriedly breaking away and making off.

But Victoire leaned all the way over the banisters, repeating softly:

"Until tomorrow. D'you hear . . . ?[4] Where are we going to be tomorrow?"

And lo and behold, the lovely sound of her voice did *not* fail in its effect, not even at *this* moment. He bounded up the stairs once more, embraced her as though saying goodbye for good, and kissed her.

"Goodbye, Mirabelle."

And listening as he went off, she still caught the sound of his steps in the hall downstairs. Then the front door clicked back into the lock and the carriage rumbled down the street.

Orderly Baarsch and the groom were seated on the box, the former having expressly asked to be allowed to drive his captain and lord of the manor on his day of glory, which had been consented to readily enough. As the carriage was turning from the Behren- into the Wilhelmstrasse, there was a jolt or jerk, even though nothing had been felt to strike the underside of the carriage.

"Damn it," said the groom. "What was that?"

"What was it? What d'you suppose it was, Tiny? A

stone, that's what it was, a dead duck of a sergeant."

"Oh no, Baarsch. Not a stone. 't was something . . . dear me . . . like shooting."

"Shooting? What the dickens."

"Yes, a pistol shot . . ."

But the sentence remained unfinished, for the carriage halted in front of Schach's house and the groom jumped down full of alarm and in haste from the box to help his master out of the carriage. He opened the carriage door, a cloud of dense smoke hit him in the face, and Schach was sitting upright in the corner, only slightly leaning back. On the rug at his feet lay the pistol. Aghast, the little groom slammed the door shut again, whimpering:

"Oh God, he's dead."

The landlord and landlady were roused, and together they carried the dead man upstairs to his lodgings.

Baarsch, swearing and crying, put the blame for everything on "mankind," because he hadn't the temerity to blame it on marriage. For he was of a diplomatic disposition like all peasants.

XX

Bülow to Sander

Königsberg
September 14, 1806

. . . You also tell me, dear Sander, about Schach. I already knew the purely factual aspect, the *Königsberg News* having briefly reported the matter, but it's only thanks to your letter that I have the explanation, insofar as one can be given. You know my tendency (which I'm also following today) to deduce the general from the particular, but also of course the other way round: the particular from the general, which is bound up with the process of generalization. This may have its drawbacks and often make me go to extremes. Still, if this approach has ever been justified, it is in this instance, and *you* will be the first to understand why this Schach case, precisely because of its implications as a symptom, has come to take such all-absorbing hold of me. It is a perfect sign of the times, though, mind you, within the limitation of its setting, a case that in its underlying causes is an altogether exceptional one. In this particular form and manifestation it could only have occurred at the seat of His Royal Majesty of Prussia's capital and court and, if beyond it, only within the ranks of our latter-day Frederickian army, an army in which honor has abdicated in favor of conceit and its soul, in favor of clockwork—a clockwork that will have run down soon enough. The Great King paved the way for this disastrous state of affairs, but things could only come to such a disastrous pass when the eyes of that Great King, which were notorious for striking greater terror into everyone's heart than combat and death, had closed for good.

I was a member of this army long enough to know that its every other word is "honor"; a dancer is charming—"on my honor"; a white steed, fabulous—"on my honor"; indeed, I had usurers recommended and introduced to me as representing the last "word of honor." And this endless chatter about honor, a bogus honor, has turned the concepts upside down and killed the real thing.

All this is also reflected in the Schach case, in Schach himself, who, for all his faults, was nevertheless one of the best.

What really were the facts of the situation? An officer is a frequent guest in a house of the aristocracy; he takes a fancy to the mother, and one fine day in May he takes a fancy to the daughter as well, perhaps—or let's say in all probability rather—because a few days before Prince Louis had treated him to a lecture on the *beauté du diable*. But be that as it may, he has taken a fancy to her, and nature arrives at the obvious conclusion. What, given these circumstances, would really have been simpler and more natural than to make amends through marriage, through a bond that would not have contravened either the practical advantage or any prejudice? But what happens? He escapes to Wuthenow, simply because the sweet creature in question is graced with a few more dimples in her cheek than happens to accord with the fashion of the day or with accepted tradition and because this "surplus of a few dimples" might have exposed our sleek Schach, polished as though by a scouring rush, to a bit of ribaldry for a month at the hands of his enemies. He escapes then, I say, beats a cowardly retreat from his obligation and commitment, and when finally, to quote his own words, his "most gracious King and Master" reminds him of his commitment and obligation and insists on implicit obedience, he obeys, but only to be guilty at the very moment of obeying of the most brusque refusal to obey. He simply can't face Zieten's mocking look, much less a new avalanche of cartoons, and thrown into a panic by a phantom, a pea-sized bubble, he resorts to the age-old expedient of the desperate: *un peu de poudre.*[1]

There you have the quintessence of hollow honor. It puts us at the mercy of the most unstable and capricious elements there are, the quicksand on which the criteria of social opinions are based, and makes us sacrifice the most sacrosanct precepts and our finest and most natural impulses on the altar of this very idol of society. And on this cult of hollow honor, which is nothing but vanity and aberration, Schach foundered, and bigger fish than he will follow suit. Mark my words. We have, ostrich-like, buried our heads in the sand so as to shut our eyes and ears. But such ostrich-like caution has never yet led to salvation. When the Ming dynasty was at the last gasp and the advance of the victorious Manchu armies had already engulfed the palace gardens of Peking, messengers and delegates kept appearing on the scene to regale the emperor with reports of victory after victory, because it was contrary to "good form" in high society and at court to speak of defeats. Oh, this business of good form! An hour later an empire was in ruins and its monarchy dethroned. And why? Because every pose leads to a lie and every lie to death.

Do you remember that evening in Frau von Carayon's drawing room where in connection with the subject of "Hannibal *ante portas*" I spoke in a similar vein? Schach scolded me at the time for being unpatriotic. Unpatriotic, indeed! Those hoisting the storm signals have always had this epithet conferred on them. And today! What I foresaw at the time as no more than a likely development has *actually* come to pass. War has been declared. And what this portends I can clearly envisage in my mind's eye. We shall be destroyed by the same world of appearances that destroyed Schach.

Yours,
Bülow

P.S. Dohna (formerly with the Garde du Corps), with whom I have just talked about the Schach affair, interprets it in a way that reminds me of Nostitz's remarks on an earlier occasion. Schach had been in love with the mother, which would have landed him, in his marriage with the daughter, in paradoxically awkward conflicts of feelings. Do write to me about this. Personally, I find it piquant, but wide of the mark. Schach's vanity left him throughout his life with complete aloofness of feeling, and his view of honor (in this context the right one for once) would, in addition, have preserved him, if he had really entered into marriage with the daughter, from any lapse.

B.

XXI

Victoire von Schach to Lisette von Perbandt

Rome
August 18, 1807

Ma chère Lisette:

I wish I could tell you how touched I was by your warm-hearted lines. Surrounded on all sides by the calamity of war, by indignities and privations, you have been overwhelmingly generous to me with manifestations of an abiding, unchanged friendship and not put an unkind interpretation on my failure to write.

Mama on more than one occasion wanted to write, but I myself asked her to wait.

Oh, my dearest Lisette, you enter full of sympathy into all that I have been through and suggest that the time has come for me to unburden myself to you. And you are right. I will do so, as best I can.

"How is one to account for it all?" you ask, adding "you were faced with a riddle that was beyond you to solve." My dear Lisette, when are riddles ever solved? They never are. A trace of the mysterious and baffling remains, and it is not given to us to peer into the ultimate and most deeply hidden mainsprings of action of others or even of ourselves. He was, so people maintain, Schach the man of good looks, and I, not to put too fine a point on it, Victoire the girl devoid of good looks—that is said to have provoked the jeers, and to bring himself to stand up to these jeers, he is supposed not to have been equal to that. And thus fear of life is said to have made him seek death.

This is how the world puts it, and there's a good deal of truth in it. He did after all write to me along similar lines and reproached himself on that score. But just as the world may have been unduly severe in its judgment, so perhaps was he in judging himself. I see it in a different light. He was perfectly aware that all the world's jeering will eventually die down and evaporate, and moreover he was man enough to defy this jeering in case it should *not* die down and *not* evaporate. No, he was not afraid of putting up a fight, or at any rate not in the way he is thought to have been. However, an astute voice, the voice of his truest and inmost self, kept relentlessly dinning it into him that he would be fighting this battle *in vain* and that even if he should win out over the world, he would not win out over himself. *That* was it. He definitely belonged to *those* men, and more so than anyone I have met, who are *not* cut out for marriage. I already told you on an earlier occasion of an outing to Tempelhof which in any case represented a turning point for us in more respects than one. On our way home from the church, we talked about knights of a religious order and the rules of such an order. And the unaffectedly serious tone in which, in spite of some bantering on my part, he treated the subject showed me clearly the ideals he felt drawn to. And these ideals—all his liaisons notwithstanding, or perhaps even because of them—certainly did not include marriage. Even now I can positively say to you, and the longing of my heart does nothing to alter this realization, that I find it difficult, indeed well-nigh impossible, to imagine him *au sein de sa famille*.[1] A cardinal (their numbers are here for me an everyday sight) simply does not fit in with the idea of a husband. And Schach doesn't either.

Now I have given you a frank account of my views, and his own thoughts and feelings must have run along similar lines, even though, to be sure, he makes no mention of this in his letter of farewell. In keeping with his whole makeup, he was bent on handling himself with panache, on asserting a certain grandeur, on largely *outward* forms, from which you may gather that I don't overestimate him. Frankly, when I saw him get the worst of it time and again in his duels with Bülow I realized only too clearly that he was a man neither of outstanding intellect nor of superior character. Granted all this; he was nevertheless able within strictly defined limits to acquit himself with flying colors and to have the upper hand. He was, as though he had been destined for it, made for the role of demigod at some princely court and would have—you mustn't laugh at this—lived up to his destiny not only to his own satisfaction, but in doing so would also have brought happiness and benefit to others, to a great many people in fact. For he was a generous person and intelligent enough, too, always to aim at generosity. In such a career of favorite and plenipotentiary at court I would have been an impediment to him, would have made him, with my simple ways, throw up whatever career he was in and driven him to Wuthenow to plant asparagus with me or to snatch an egg from under the sitting hen. Such a prospect filled him with alarm. He saw a confined and parochial life stretching ahead of him and was out for, I won't say an ambitious one, but all the same for one that struck *him* as ambitious.

My lack of beauty he would have been able to take in his stride. I didn't actually—I almost hesitate to write it down—displease him, and perhaps he really did love me. If I am to go by his last lines, he truly did. But I distrust this beguiling word. For he was full of tenderness and compassion, and all the grief he had caused me by his life and his death he was anxious to assuage, insofar as it could be assuaged.

All the grief! Oh, with what an alien and reproachful look this word stares at me. No, my dear Lisette, let's be done with grief. I had early on come to accept resignation and imagined I had no right to the most glorious thing that life has to offer. And now I have known it. Love. How it lifts up my spirits and sets me quivering from head to foot, transforming all grief into bliss. There lies the child, whose eyes are opening this very moment. *His* eyes. No, Lisette, I have had to contend with a heavy burden, but it vanishes gracefully into thin air when weighed against my happiness.

The little one, your little godchild, was ill, on the verge of death, and I was allowed to keep it only by a miracle.

And I must tell you about it.

When the doctor had come to the end of his resources, I went with our landlady (a true Roman of the old school in her dignity and kindness of heart) up to the church of Ara Coeli, an old building with round arches by the Capitol where they keep the *bambino*, the Christ child, a wooden doll in swaddling clothes with large eyes made of glass and a veritable diadem of headbands, the gifts of countless mothers to the Christ child in gratitude for his help. I had brought a headband with me even before I could be sure of his intercession, and the *bambino* must have been touched by this gesture of faith. For lo, he did help. A crisis presently developed, and the *dottore* announced his *va bene*,[2] while the landlady smiled as if she had worked the miracle herself.

And in this connection I wonder what Aunt Marguerite, if she were told of this, would have to say about all this "superstition." She would warn me of the old church and with *more* justification than she knows.

For Ara Coeli is not merely *old*, but also a source of solace and succor, and cool and beautiful.

But what is most beautiful about it is its name, which means "Altar of Heaven." And from this altar ascends my daily offering of thanks.

Notes

1

1. *frondeurs:* Opponents of the policies pursued by the successors of Frederick the Great.
2. Bülow: Heinrich Dietrich von Bülow (1757–1807), writer on military and political affairs. Fontane drew on his *Der Feldzug von 1805* (*The Campaign of 1805*).
3. Haugwitz: Count Christian von Haugwitz (1752–1832), Prussian statesman; had signed the treaties with Napoleon at Schönbrunn (December 15, 1805; rejected by Berlin), Paris (February 15, 1806) for Prussia's enforced alliance with France in exchange for Hanover, which was linked to the British Crown.
4. postnuptial gift: According to an old German custom, a husband would give his wife, on the morning after the wedding, a present known as a *Morgengabe.*
5. between the Nuthe and Notte: The Berlin area bounded by these two rivers.
6. Kalenberg: Fertile region along the Leine on which Hanover is situated.
7. And Vienna of all places: John III of Poland was instrumental in raising the siege of Vienna by the Turks in 1683 with a contingent of Polish troops.
8. His Majesty: Frederick William III of Prussia (reigned 1797–1840).
9. *imperator;* the Emperor; *empéreur:* Napoleon.
10. the great King: Frederick the Great.

II

1. Rahel Levin: 1771–1833; her salon in Berlin was renowned as a gathering place for leading German and French writers and philosophers; married the publicist and diplomat Karl Varnhagen von Ense.
2. the Prince: Prince Louis Ferdinand of Prussia (1772–1806), leader of the war party; killed in combat shortly before the battle of Jena. Fontane wrote a ballad about him.
3. *The Consecration of Strength: Die Weihe der Kraft*, a play by the German Romantic playwright Zacharias Werner (1768–1823), first performed in Berlin in June, 1806.
4. *regarder dans le néant:* To look into the void.
5. Iffland: August Wilhelm Iffland (1759–1814), prominent actor, theater manager, and playwright.
6. *Pectus facit oratorem:* It's the heart that makes the speaker (Quintilian).
7. when the purple drops . . . : From Schiller's tragedy, *Die Verschwörung des Fiesco zu Genua (The Conspiracy of Fiesco at Genoa.)* The usurper duke, his robe torn off, is pushed into the sea.
8. *Hannibal ante portas:* Hannibal before the gates, i.e., the enemy is close at hand (in allusion to the warning alerting Rome to the Carthaginian general's seemingly imminent approach in 211 B.C.).
9. I tied him to the crib . . . : Marginal note by Frederick the Great on a petition by an army quartermaster's widow for a pension.

III

1. Look, fortunes lies . . . : From Goethe's quatrain "Erinnerung" ("Reflection").
2. asperula . . . : Woodruff, after Carl Linnaeus (1707–78), Swedish botanist.
3. Nostitz: Karl von Nostitz (1781–1838), aide-de-camp to Prince Louis. His memoirs were an important source for Fontane, especially for Chapter XI.
4. Französisch-Buchholz: Formerly village northwest of Berlin, Huguenot settlement in the days of the Great Elector.

5. *C'est le premier pas* . . . : It's the first step that is difficult.
6. *Hâtez-vous:* Hurry up.

IV

1. hyperboreans: Inhabitants of the far north.
2. Princesse Charlotte/Alexandrine: Daughters of Frederick William III.
3. *l'exactitude* . . . : Punctuality is the politeness of kings.
4. Count von der Mark: Died as a boy; son of Frederick William II by his mistress (see note 3, Chapter XVI, p. 201).
5. There's naught so finely spun . . . : /But is cometh to the sun.
6. *Un teint de lys et de rose:* A fair complexion (lilies and roses).
7. Ulm/Austerlitz: Surrender to the French by the Austrian General Mack at Ulm, October 20, 1805, opening the way for Napoleon to enter Vienna before his victory over the Russians and Austrians at Austerlitz, December 2, 1805.
8. Brunswick: Duke Charles William Ferdinand of Brunswick (1735–1806), commanded Prussian and Austrian troops against revolutionary France (1792–7); mortally wounded fighting Napoleon's forces at Auerstädt.
9. Hohenlohe: General Prince Frederick Louis of Hohenlohe (1746–1818), fought against revolutionary France and Napoleon; defeated at Jena.
10. Knight Templar: Member of a religious military order among the Crusaders dating from the early 12th century to protect pilgrims and the Holy Sepulcher.
11. Russian general: The commander of the Russian detachment occupying Berlin in October, 1760.
12. Fehrbellin: Battle of Fehrbellin, June 28, 1675, in which the Great Elector of Brandenburg defeated the Swedes.
13. Philip the Fair: Philip IV of France (reigned 1285–1314); compelled Pope Clement V to suppress the Templars in 1312, himself appropriating their wealth.

V

1. Massenbach and Phull: Writers on military affairs, opposed to a hard-line policy toward Napoleon.

VI

1. Moabit: Today part of northwest Berlin.
2. *A la guerre . . . :* I.e., we must take the rough with the smooth.
3. *Ah, ces Prussiens . . . :* Ah, these Prussians are even more stupid than the Austrians.
4. Lombard: Ministerial adviser to Haugwitz; of Huguenot extraction; advocated accommodation with Napoleon.
5. *L'hirondelle frise . . . /rase . . . :* The swallow brushes (curls)/ skims (shaves) the surface of the water.
6. Lehwald: Prussian general in the Seven Years' War.
7. *Hic haeret:* There's the catch.
8. Kutuzov: Michael Ilarionovich Kutuzov (1745–1813), Russian field marshal; commanded the Russo-Austrian troops at Austerlitz; denied Moscow to Napoleon by the battle of Borodino in 1812.
9. There's a passage somewhere . . . : From a ballad by Gottfried August Bürger (1747–94).
10. Czar's visit: Alexander I's state visit in November 1805.
11. *deliciae generis humanae:* From the Roman historian Suetonis's description of the Emperor Titus—"the darling of mankind."
12. Cross of St. Andrew: The highest Russian decoration.
13. Brenkenhof: Served under Frederick the Great; consultant and writer on economic affairs.
14. last king of Poland: Stanislas II (1732–98). His abdication in 1795 marked the end of Poland's weak elective monarchy.
15. *beauté coquette . . . :* Coquettish, commonplace, celestial, satanic beauty, and beauty which alone inspires genuine feeling.

VII

1. Dussek: Jan Ladislav Dussek (1760–1812), Bohemian-born pianist and composer; music teacher to Prince Louis, 1803–06.
2. *Mieux vaut tard . . . :* Better late than never.
3. homage to the arts: Allusion to a play by Schiller with that title, *Huldigung der Künste.*
4. *Parturiunt montes . . . :* The mountains will be in labor (only) to bring forth a ridiculous mouse. (Horace, *Ars Poetica.*)

5. *Chi va piano* ... : Who walks softly walks safely.
6. Rüchel: General; proponent of antiquated military views.
7. Kalckreuth: Prussian general and field marshal (1737–1818); received the rarely awarded Black Eagle (a higher decoration than the Red) late in his career.
8. my good friend Pauline: Pauline Wiesel, wife of a Prussian official, inamorata of Prince Louis, and friendly with Rahel Levin.
9. Massov's children's ball: Massov was minister of state and royal marshal whose children's balls were celebrated affairs.
10. our Gentz: Friedrich von Gentz (1764–1832), publicist and politician, transferred from Prussian to Austrian diplomatic service, strongly anti-Napoleon; adviser to Metternich, Secretary General of the Congress of Vienna.
11. Buchholz: Historian and publicist critical of existing conditions and the anti-Napoleon faction.
12. *Mais revenons* ... : But to return to our fair Victoire.
13. *Comme un ange:* Like an angel.
14. *restitutio in integrum:* Restoration to the former immaculate state.
15. Morgarten and Sempach: Swiss peasants' victories in 1315 and 1386 respectively, ridding themselves of Hapsburg rule.
16. *toujours perdrix:* Forever partridge (can be too much of a good thing).
17. *le laid* ... : Cp. "Fair is foul, and foul is fair" (*Macbeth*, I).
18. *sine umbra:* I.e., casting no shadow.

VIII

1. Prague and Leuthen: Victories of Frederick the Great in 1757.
2. Valmy and Pirmasens: Defeat of the Prussians and Austrians in 1792 and victory of the Prussians in 1793 respectively in the War of the First Coalition against revolutionary France.
3. *Wallenstein, The Maid of Orleans, William Tell:* Plays by Schiller.
4. *Holberg's Political Tinker:* Satirical comedy by the "Danish Molière," Ludvig Holberg (1684–1754).
5. *cercle intime:* Private gathering.
6. Because I feel a greater affinity for him: Mirabeau, whose aims as a moderate constitutionalist in the Revolution remained unrealized, was left scarred by smallpox.

7. What are you upset about?: Schach, significantly at this point, for the first and only time addresses Victoire by the familiar *du*, while she continues to use the polite form, *Sie*. (Cp. note 4 for Chapter XIX below.)

IX

1. Katharina von Bora: Married Luther in 1525 after adopting his doctrines and escaping from a convent.

X

1. Radziwills and Carolaths: Prominent aristocratic families.
2. famous general: Cavalry General von Zieten (1699–1786), "Old Father Zieten," achieved fame in the Seven Years' War.
3. *lupus in fabula:* The wolf in the fable (i.e., talk of the devil and he's sure to appear).
4. *C'est pours les domestiques./ Et pour la canaille:* That's for the servants to see to./ And for the rabble.

XI

1. *bel étage:* The then fashionable first floor above ground level.

XII

1. cutting of Victoire's garter: The bride's garter, according to established custom among the nobility, was cut into small pieces which were divided among the guests as a memento.

XIV

1. Sans Souci: ["Free from care."] The palace at Potsdam built in 1745–48 to Frederick the Great's specifications, inspired by Versailles. It ranks as one of the celebrated examples of German rococo.

2. the old Princess: Mother of Prince Louis.
3. *Est-elle riche* . . . : Is she rich? Undoubtedly. I understand.
4. Malplaquet: Defeat of the French by Prince Eugene of Savoy and Marlborough (1709).
5. *Hochkirch:* In Saxony. Scene of a successful Austrian surprise attack on Frederick the Great's forces in 1758 (Seven Years' War).

XV

1. *Obodrite descent:* Old dynasty and people tracing their ancestry to the northern Slavs in medieval Europe; became Germanized and inhabited what is now Mecklenburg.
2. farmer-general's daughter: The farmers-general in eighteenth-century France were an association of financiers who, on the strength of their loans to the Crown, were entitled to collect (farm) the indirect taxes on behalf of the Crown at enormous profit both to themselves and to their agents. The Revolution, when many of them were guillotined, put an end to this practice.
3. *ces pauvres gens* . . . : Those poor people, those unfortunate Carayons.
4. *Gironde* . . . *the Mountain:* The Girondists, mainly from the Gironde region in southwest France, were moderate republicans; suppressed in 1793, their prominent members were executed by the Jacobins, the radicals seated up high on the "Mountain" in the National Assembly.
5. *the Lusignans:* Old French dynasty in Cypress, which they acquired during the Crusades. Melusine, their founder and tutelary fairy in French romance, married Raymond, Count of Lusignan, but vanished when he discovered her transformed into part woman and part serpent.

XVI

1. *Frederick William II:* reigned 1786–97.
2. *Hufeland:* Physician and university professor.
3. *Frau Rietz* . . . : Variant names of mistress of Frederick William II and mother of Count von der Mark (see p. 38).

4. *Bischofswerder:* He was known for his spiritualistic practices at the court of Frederick William II.
5. *Que vous êtes bon* . . . : How kind of you, my dear General.
6. *Correggio:* (1494?–1534); possibly his *Noli me tangere* (Prado, Madrid).

XVII

1. Turkish Pavilion: A café.
2. Marienfliess or Heiligengrabe: Former convents which, after the Reformation, were turned into homes for unmarried daughters of the nobility and run along hierarchical, quasi-religious institutional lines.
3. *et payer les pots cassés:* And pay for the broken pots.

XVIII

1. Fata Morgana: A mirage produced by reflections from the sea, especially near the Strait of Messina, so named from Morgan le Fay, sorceress sister of King Arthur, said to dwell in Calabria.
2. Bridge of Sighs: Covered passageway between the Doges' Palace and the prison in Venice over which those condemned to death were led sighing.
3. Islands of the Sirens: From where, in Homer's *Odyssey*, the two sirens lured sailors to their death by seductive singing, a fate Ulysses escaped by filling his companions' ears with wax and having himself lashed to the mast of his ship.

XIX

1. farmers-general: See note 2 for Chapter XV.
2. sacred bird of Egypt: The sacred ibis of the ancient Egyptians, related to the stork.
3. *on revient toujours* . . . : One always returns to one's first love.
4. D'you hear . . . : This is the only time that Victoire uses the familiar *du* in addressing Schach. (He himself had used it once; see note 7 Chapter VIII.)

XX

1. *un peu de poudre:* A little powder, i.e., gun powder.
2. Ming dynasty: 1368–1644; succeeded by the invading Manchus.

XXI

1. *au sein de sa famille:* In the bosom of his family.
2. *va bene:* Doing nicely.

Bibliography

In preparing the translation, Introduction, and Notes I have had the benefit of two annotated and documented German editions of the novel: Gotthard Erler's in Volume 3 of Fontane's *Romane und Erzählungen* (Berlin & Weimar, 1969) and Pierre-Paul Sagave's (Frankfurt & Berlin, 1966). I have also consulted the edition of Edgar Gross in Volume 2 of Fontaine's *Sämtliche Werke* (Munich, 1959–).

Works by Fontane available in English include the following:

FICTION

Beyond Recall (*Unwiederbringlich*), tr. by Douglas Parmée; London, 1964.
Effi Briest, tr. & abr. by William A. Cooper; New York, 1966.
Effi Briest, tr. by Douglas Parmée; London, 1967.
A Suitable Match (*Irrungen, Wirrungen*), tr. by Sandra Morris; London & Glasgow, 1968.
"A Woman of My Age" ("Eine Frau in meinen Jahren"), tr. by E. M. Valk, *Transatlantic Review*, 37/38; London & New York, 1970–71.

NONFICTION

Across the Tweed: A Tour of Mid-Victorian Scotland (*Jenseits des Tweed*), tr. by Brian Battershaw; London, 1965.

Some critical studies in English of Fontane:

Garland, H. B., "Theodor Fontane," *German Men of Letters*, ed. by Alex Natan; London, 1961.

Hatfield, Henry, "The Renovation of the German Novel: Theodor Fontane," *Crisis and Continuity in Modern German Fiction*; Ithaca, N.Y., 1969.

Hayens, Kenneth, *Theodor Fontane*; London, 1920.

Pascal, Roy, "Theodor Fontane," *The German Novel*; Manchester, 1956; London, 1965.

Rowley, Brian A., "Theodor Fontane: A German Novelist in the European Tradition?" *German Life and Letters*, 15, 1961.

Samuel, Richard, "Theodor Fontane," *Selected Writings*; Melbourne, 1965.

Stern, J. P., "Theodor Fontane: The Realism of Assessment," *Idylls and Realities*; London & New York, 1972.

Some German studies of Fontane:

Brinkmann, Richard, *Theodor Fontane: Über die Verbindlichkeit des Unverbindlichen*; Munich, 1967.

Demetz, Peter, *Formen des Realismus: Theodor Fontane*; Munich, 1964.

Jolles, Charlotte, *Theodor Fontane* (Metzler series, *Realien zur Literatur*, M 114); Stuttgart, 1972.

Lukács, Georg, "Der alte Fontane," *Deutsch Realisten des 19. Jahrhunderts*; Berlin, 1951.

Martini, Fritz, "Theodor Fontane," *Deutsche Literatur im bürgerlichen Realismus*; Stuttgart, 1964.

Müller-Seidel, Walter, "Gesellschaft und Menschlichkeit im Roman von Theodor Fontane," *Heidelberger Jahrbuch*, 4, 1960.

Nürnberger, Helmuth, *Theodor Fontane in Selbstzeugnissen und Bilddokumenten*; Hamburg, 1968.

Reuter, Heinrich, *Fontane* (2 vols.); Munich, 1968.

Richter, Karl, *Resignation: Eine Studie zum Werk Theodor Fontanes*; Stuttgart, 1966.